"Estes' debut novel traces the r
ordered life as dream and rea
Fanciful reading..." *Kirkus Di*

What readers across the country are saying about *Plane of the Ecliptic*...

"This book grabbed my attention from the first couple of pages and it never let me go. I am recommending it to all of my friends and have given two copies as gifts."

—Barbara J. McDonald, Pleasanton, CA

"For me, a worthwhile book stirs up many emotions. *Plane of the Ecliptic* did exactly that!"

—Ginger Suriano Myers, Spokane, WA

"I was hooked from the first page and all the way through to the end. The author has a wonderful way of drawing you into her characters and making you feel a part of their lives. A GREAT read!"

—Mary Ann McDonald, Keller, TX

"Karen Estes captures the everyday life experiences of her main character, Maggie, in crisp, precise, imaginative prose. Maggie is real -- she became a friend I cheered on throughout her journey. *Plane of the Ecliptic* is a captivating creation."

—Brenda Prowse, Poulsbo, WA

"The author's unique way of writing kept me practically speed reading the whole way through. I loved that I could relate to the main character but not predict what would happen next."

—Pat McDonald, Lake Oswego, OR

"Karen Estes has created a suspense-filled story that keeps you guessing about the outcome until the final chapter. My book club chose *Plane of the Ecliptic* as one of our monthly selections and enjoyed a fascinating discussion."

—Nancy Bufalo, St. Louis, MO

"*Plane of the Ecliptic* is a perfect book for grandmothers, mothers, and daughters. It has a little bit of everything - mystery, humor, spirituality, and intrigue. We highly recommend it for anyone looking for a fresh, cleverly written story."

—Kimberly Shaddox and Samantha Loete, Hayden, ID

For a link to book club discussion questions,
visit www.PlaneoftheEcliptic.com

Plane of the Ecliptic

Karen Estes

Karen Estes

iUniverse, Inc.
New York   Bloomington

Plane of the Ecliptic

iUniverse books may be ordered through booksellers or by contacting:

iUniverse
1663 Liberty Drive
Bloomington, IN 47403
www.iuniverse.com
1-800-Authors (1-800-288-4677)

Because of the dynamic nature of the Internet, any Web addresses or links contained in this book may have changed since publication and may no longer be valid. The views expressed in this work are solely those of the author and do not necessarily reflect the views of the publisher, and the publisher hereby disclaims any responsibility for them.

ISBN: 978-1-4401-8912-8 (sc)
ISBN: 978-1-4401-8910-4 (dj)
ISBN: 978-1-4401-8911-1 (ebk)

Library of Congress Control Number: 2009911758

Printed in the United States of America

iUniverse rev. date: 10/25/2010

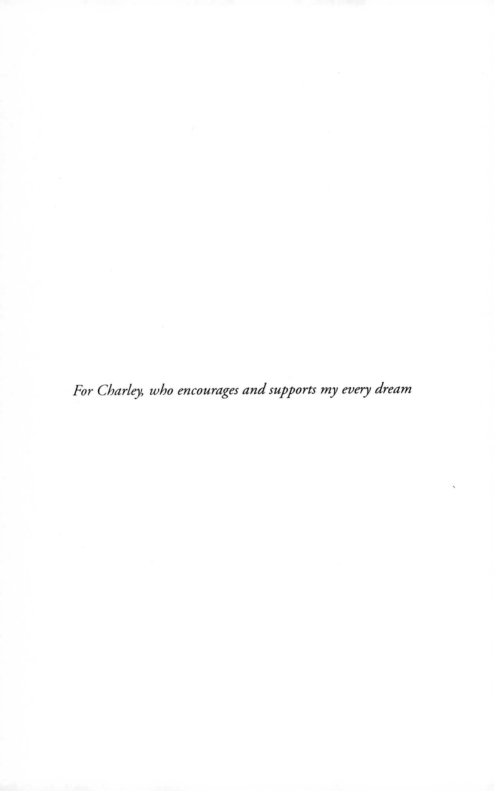

For Charley, who encourages and supports my every dream

Prologue

A fresh innocence glistened in the eyes of the five-year-old girl, as her hair flew wildly in the spring breeze. Oblivious of her own charm, she appeared all the more captivating to the woman walking slowly toward her through the meadow.

"Here you are, sweetheart." She handed the girl a single flower picked from the hundreds just like it in the field.

As the girl raised her face, the woman was stunned to see her full, rosy cheeks wet with tears. She knelt beside her, gathered her in her arms, and stroked the wind-blown hair until the child was calm.

"I'm afraid." The little girl's voice was both confident and quivering.

"Afraid? Afraid of what?"

Desperate to remain in the woman's embrace, the girl pulled away just enough to see her eyes. "Of being without you," she said. "I'm afraid I will get lost from you, or you will get lost from me."

"Oh, but that will never be," the woman assured her.

"But what if it does happen? What shall I do?"

The woman smiled and brushed a wisp of hair away from the girl's temple. "Even when we're apart, I'll never leave you."

"How will I know?" the girl persisted.

"When the time and place are right, you'll know."

Relief finally began to show on the girl's face. "Promise me?"

"I promise."

The woman stood, reached for the girl's hand, and pulled her to her feet. Their dresses settled gently around their legs, each skirt swirling in search of the other as they walked along together. The girl, satisfied for now, carried the flower tightly in her free hand, as if it would help her remember the woman's comforting words. But slowly, the unrelenting wind released the white petals, one after another, until all that was left was the golden center.

Part 1

Our truest life is when we are in dreams awake.

—Henry David Thoreau

Chapter 1

It was just as well she didn't know. A crucial form of protection really—not realizing what the future held. She would have only begun fretting that much earlier, which wouldn't have made the slightest bit of difference to anyone involved. The outcome would remain the same, no matter what. Consequently, since forthcoming events were as inconspicuous as the hyacinth bulbs hidden beneath the lingering March snow in her front yard, Maggie set about the evening routine with her usual resolve.

The clock glowed a red 9:35 after she had double-checked the alarm setting, and she and Ross had turned off their respective nightstand lights—Maggie's a hollow glass lamp filled with seashells, Ross's a carved wooden golden retriever head. In his exhausted and blissful state of puppyhood, Spencer snored on his fleece bed. Cleo claimed a place atop the comforter near Maggie's feet, kneading with her front paws and purring. Ross kissed Maggie. They uttered simultaneous good nights and rolled over, shoulders, backs, and rear ends aligned against each other just the way they liked it. Everything was exactly the same as the night before and the night before that.

Then the phone rang.

Maggie answered it. She had barely said hello when Kellie shouted, "Mom? I need your help!"

Maggie held the receiver away from her ear and turned on the seashell lamp, yawning. Kellie wasn't due for another three weeks, and Maggie suspected she was experiencing a severe case of heartburn, a condition she managed to develop almost every other night. It reminded Maggie of the year Kellie turned five and contracted a chronic case of hiccups in anticipation of starting kindergarten.

"What is it, honey?" Maggie hoped a quick word of reassurance would be all Kellie needed, and she could return to her comfortable bed next to Ross. She couldn't possibly face all those teenagers at school tomorrow without a full eight hours of sleep.

"Only that the baby's coming and I'm not ready," Kellie screamed in between dramatic huffs and puffs.

For the duration of Kellie's pregnancy, Maggie had helped her through morning sickness, mood swings, sleepless nights, and a belly stretched as tight as plastic wrap over a bowl. She accompanied her to all of her doctor's visits, and consoled her after each weigh-in. She provided Kellie with all the latest pregnancy and child-rearing books, assuring her that no mother on the planet knew exactly the right thing to do every second of her child's life. Now, however, Maggie tried desperately to disguise the anxiety bubbling in her own stomach.

"Oh, but, sweetheart, this isn't according to the schedule. Your due date's not until April 2."

"Well, apparently we neglected to tell this baby about the schedule." Kellie let out what sounded like a mother bear's growl, followed by heavy breathing mixed with wretched moans of pain.

"Where are you?"

"Sean is just warming up the car. Meet us at the hospital as fast as you can." Kellie squeaked. "You won't get a ticket, Mom, I promise. Ohh … I can't believe this!"

"I'll be there."

Maggie carefully placed the phone back in its charger and looked around the bedroom, half-expecting someone to jump out, gleefully telling her this was all a practical joke. Brow furrowed in concentration, she stepped into the bathroom and brushed her teeth one more time by the pale glow of the nightlight. Choosing her moss green slacks and matching cashmere sweater with the little collar and three pearl buttons, she took a look in the mirror. The sweater brought out a tiny bit of green in her hazel eyes. She smiled as she reached for a brush to fluff her short dark hair. *Everything will be fine,* she thought. *Everything will be fine.*

"Are you going to tell me what's going on?"

Ross's voice startled her. She'd forgotten he was barely ten feet away.

"Oh, it was only Kellie. She thinks she might be in labor, but it's probably heartburn. I told her I'd meet her at the hospital just in case." Saying all this out loud to her husband made it seem logical and true.

Ross propped himself up on his elbow, running his free hand through his dark hair, unconsciously covering up the balding spot. "I'm coming with you."

"Fine, but I'm driving." She handed Ross his pants.

Deep in slumber, Spencer twitched his paws. Cleo remained in position, undoubtedly anticipating the eventual return of Maggie's feet.

Once in the car, Maggie drove as fast as her follow-the-rules-no-matter-what nature would allow. Kellie, as close to Maggie as a stepdaughter could possibly be, knew her well enough to hint it would be okay to go slightly over the speed limit in this situation. And in spite of being caught off guard, Maggie reminded herself she was fully prepared. Weeks ago, she'd memorized the quickest route between home and the hospital, as well as between school and the hospital. Oh yes, and between the Marketfresh grocery store and the hospital. No need to take any chances figuring all that out at the last minute. At least most of the evidence of the late spring snowstorm that had hit Summerhill two weeks earlier was gone. Sloppy piles of dirty snow stood on every corner, but the streets themselves were in fine shape. Certainly there was no reason at all to worry about icy conditions. She held the accelerator steady.

They found the emergency room in sheer chaos. How could anyone work in such makeshift conditions? Frazzled people in colorful scrubs ran here and there. Small, tired children whimpered near a tall woman holding a once yellow towel to her bleeding temple. Oddly, two teenaged boys stared at a rerun of *Little House on the Prairie*, close to tearing up right along with Michael Landon. A desk nurse, the only person who seemed happy to be in there, scanned her stack of paperwork and promptly announced Kellie and Sean were already in their birthing room. Third floor.

Still convinced this was merely a false alarm, Maggie guided Ross by the elbow into the next free elevator, straightening her sweater as the doors closed.

In the labor and delivery wing, they were ushered into room 310, only to find a frightened young man, blonde curls falling around his face, leaning over Kellie's bed.

"Is that our son-in-law?" Ross blurted. But there was no time for anyone to answer.

"What took you so long, Mom?" Kellie demanded between pants. "You know I can't have this baby without you and— Oh, my God, it's pushing, it's pushing!"

Shocked by the expansive distance between her stepdaughter's knees, Maggie switched mental gears. Apparently her initial heartburn hypothesis no longer applied. She couldn't help but notice Kellie had leaped far beyond the particular childbirth class that taught the expectant mothers how to breathe in and out, when to breathe in and out, and how to continually adapt the in and out breathing to work with the "natural process of birth." Yes, the natural childbirth ship had already sailed.

"Now that you're both here," said Sean, "maybe I'll just wait in the hallway." His look of relief rivaled the one Maggie had witnessed on Ross's face when he discovered he would not be the featured speaker at the Washington Society of Certified Public Accountants after all.

"Oh no, you don't," Kellie shrieked. "Seeing as it's apparently too late for any high-powered drugs, there's no way I'm going through this by myself." Reaching for the front of Sean's shirt, she snarled through gritted teeth, "Don't you dare move."

Maggie suddenly noticed a nurse checking Kellie—a nurse who, thankfully, seemed confidently in charge of the entire event. Jeannie, as her name tag proclaimed, cradled Kellie's knee in her arm, calmly instructing her how to breathe and push at every appropriate moment. A second nurse set up a cart of assorted instruments, while a third prepared an isolette. "This is a sterile tray," Jeannie declared, as she adjusted it into place with one gloved hand. "Try not to touch it."

Mouth hanging open, Sean stared at the sterile off-limits cart, which not only had been positioned directly in front of him, but also signified the urgency of the situation. He looked frantically between the three nurses and Kellie. "But it's all happening so fast!" he howled and collapsed in the chair beside his wife's bed.

Jeannie's mouth turned up slightly at the corner. "Sometimes this is just how it happens. We've apparently got one who is simply determined to join the world."

Totally unaccustomed to any level of lack of control, Maggie felt overwhelmed at the hasty sequence of events. Consequently, she loved this nurse already. Reaching for the cool, damp washcloth lying in the plastic tray near the bed, she held it against her own face. "Ross, honey, would you please go down the hall and buy me a bottle of water?"

Ross didn't argue. He practically ran out of the room just as Kellie let out an unsettling high-pitched yelp.

"Uh-oh," Jeannie muttered. "We're going to have a baby with the next push. I don't think your doctor will have time to get here."

One of the other nurses reached for her pager. "I'll call down to ER."

Jeannie took her place at the end of the bed. "All right, Kellie, deep breath. Now push, push, push!"

Maggie's face flushed scarlet right along with Kellie's, as mother and daughter held their breath and pushed together. While Sean cautiously peered through his fingers, Jeannie announced, "We have a beautiful girl."

The nurse wiped down the gooey red baby before placing her gently on Kellie's tummy. "May I present your brand-new daughter."

The infant, so insistent on coming early, wailed as if yearning for the cozy, safe harbor of her mother's womb. One of the other nurses, heated blanket in hand, skillfully rubbed and cleaned the baby, all the while moving her closer to her mother's face. "Isn't she gorgeous?" she asked.

"You were amazing, honey," Maggie said, brushing Kellie's damp hair away from her forehead.

"Yeah, you did great," mumbled Sean. "I wish it hadn't all happened so fast, though. There wasn't even time to sit in the Jacuzzi over there."

Ross stood in the doorway with a bottle of water. "A girl. Imagine that." Kellie and Sean had been determined to let the baby's gender be a surprise. Anticipating a boy nevertheless, Ross had spent two hours at Toys R Us looking at fire trucks and toddler-sized fishing poles last week. But now, of course, it didn't matter. "I'm thrilled, Kellie, I really am."

Sheepishly, over the baby's deafening cry, Sean said, "I'm glad I stayed. It was pretty amazing."

"Yes, it was." Maggie knew she drove Sean nuts most of the time. All her rules, regulations, and particular ways of doing things were usually more than he could handle. Sean was not necessarily the son-in-law she would have chosen, but tonight she willingly let that go.

Another hour zipped by before anyone realized it. Nurse Jeannie briefly moved the baby to a warming area, where she fastened a pink identification bracelet on her wrist. Ross and Sean seized the opportunity to count fingers and toes. But Maggie, for some unknown reason, kept her distance. Through all of this, even through Kellie's attempt to nurse her, the baby cried until her little body turned purple.

"Don't worry, honey," Jeannie assured Kellie. "It's nothing you're doing. She's absolutely normal and will calm down any minute. Birth can be more traumatic for some babies than others, that's all."

"Mom, do you want to hold her? I don't know what else she needs." Frustrated, Kellie leaned back against her pillow, the howling baby still in the crook of her arm.

Maggie hesitantly stepped up to the edge of the bed. She hadn't held a baby since her friend Claire had shown off her new grandson two years before. As if transporting a rare orchid, Maggie gently carried the infant to the padded bench near the window in the back of the room.

"I'll sit with Kellie while she rests," she vaguely heard Ross say.

A cloud moved aside just then, making way for the dazzling full moon to illuminate this woman and newborn, like a spotlight on the lead characters in a play. Maggie pulled back the soft blanket for a better glimpse. Her eyes locked with the puffy blue ones peering out of the small bundle as she reached for the tiny braceleted hand. A level of semi-consciousness, resembling that of waking from a pleasant afternoon nap, consumed them both as the crying, along with all of the surrounding tension, was replaced with the faraway sound of a flute. Or possibly chiming bells. Emotions that would take years to explain, or even admit to, arose within the depths of Maggie's being. The unfamiliar sensation was either bafflingly wrong or clearly right. She thought of calling out across the room, and tried to open her mouth. But speaking proved unnecessary, as the connection between her and this fresh soul intensified, held fast, and inevitably recognized something long forgotten.

It was just moments before midnight, the first day of spring.

Chapter 2

A heavy wooden door creaks open. Near the corner of the room stands a small dark-haired girl. Her father motions for a bearded man and a red-headed girl to hurry in. Freezing wind and snow blow into the house. Together the men push the door closed again.

"We've been expecting ye," says the dark-haired girl's father. "Come in out o' the blizzard." He steps forward to shake the bearded man's hand. "And who might this young lass be?"

"Hopin' it wouldna be any trouble to bring along me daughter. Her mam has all she can handle with the twins and the newest wee one. This lassie begged to come with me."

The girls walk toward each other, smiling. Red-head takes off a woven straw bracelet and holds it out. "I made it," she says.

"Oh, 'tis bonnie!" The dark-haired girl slips it over her wrist.

"There be plenty o' mutton stew for all." A woman smiles shyly at the guests as she stirs a kettle. Her cheeks are rosy from the steam. She fans her face with her apron and smoothes away wisps of auburn hair. "And flakey baps too."

Two young boys run out from a back room. Wooden chairs scrape against the stone floor. All sit down and bow their heads.

"Heavenly Father, thank ye for the food before us. Look over us in the days to come as we work to unite our great country. Thank ye for our new friends who have ridden far to be with us. Amen." The father looks up, dips out a bowl of stew, and hands it to the bearded man.

The girls scoot closer together. Grinning, they reach for each other's hands.

Maggie sat up in bed, her heart pounding like the beat of a familiar tune stuck in her head. Only she couldn't recall the name of this particular song, the lyrics beyond her grasp. What kind of dream was this?

She glanced over at Ross. He lay on his right side, covers pushed down to his waist, one arm flung across his face. They'd only been grandparents for a few hours, but he was already exhausted.

Although the clock said 4:11, much earlier than Maggie usually started her day, she put on her fleece robe and crept downstairs to make the coffee. Once in the kitchen, she navigated by the shimmering glow of the moon shining through the window over the sink. Breathing deeply and deliberately, she attempted to calm the uneasy shiver running down her back.

Chapter 3

In spite of the curious experience at the hospital on Thursday evening and the unsettling dream later that night, Maggie took special care to begin each of the subsequent days as she always did—one cup of coffee while reading the newspaper, twenty minutes of stretching, yoga, and deep breathing, and then shower, hair, and makeup. The latter two routines consisted of a dollop of mousse evenly distributed through her short dark hair, one or two minutes with the dryer, non-comedogenic moisturizer, light foundation, and a single coat of mascara. For breakfast she ate her usual low-fat yogurt with a sliced banana and one cup of Raisin Bran. Floss, brush, a touch of Revlon Twinkled Pink lipstick, and ready to go. Although notably anxious inside, Maggie saw no point in changing any part of her ritual at this point.

On Monday morning, she pulled into her parking space at Summerhill High School, her home for the past seventeen years. The thirty-six-year-old two-story brick building stood with the flag flying in front of the office and football field behind the gym, quiet now except for the track team running and jumping every afternoon. These familiar sights, common to most high schools in America, reassured her that the world was just the same as it had been a few days ago. She checked her mailbox slot in the office, smiled at everyone, and exchanged the usual "How was your weekend?" and "Good morning." After squeezing her royal blue thermal lunch bag into the staff refrigerator, she walked down the hall to the library and shut the door. Amazingly, the library had not changed.

The substitute covering for her on Friday had left everything in perfect order. Ron Chapman was a retired English teacher Maggie had taken a chance on three years before. Reliable substitutes were hard to find. Frequently, they had no experience in the school system, thinking it would be a quick and easy way to earn a few bucks. Ron, however, with his tidy crew cut, thick black-rimmed glasses, and pressed tie, commanded discipline. He turned out to be an absolute gem when Maggie needed an occasional day off. Not only did he abide by her detailed plans, he mastered the computer circulation system, picked up on small projects waiting to be completed, and considered every book he placed in the hands of a student a personal success story. Luckily, Ron had been available when Maggie woke him with a 6:00 AM phone call on Friday morning.

Too confused over her unusual experiences to help Kellie and Sean take their new daughter home on Saturday, Maggie startled everyone by insisting the new parents settle in by themselves for the weekend. She said she wanted Kellie and Sean to have some time alone with the baby, but volunteered to deliver dinner on Monday night. That would be best, Maggie maintained. And, as usual, the family all relied on her to know what was best.

She secretly hoped the extra time would help her figure out exactly what had happened the night her granddaughter was born.

Relieved to be back in her safe, predictable library, Maggie picked up a marker and started writing the daily trivia on the small dry erase board next to the computerized card catalog.

Halfway through second period, Joey Martinez tapped Maggie on the shoulder. "Mrs. MacKenzie, are you okay?"

"Huh?" Maggie forced herself to focus on the boy dressed in charcoal jeans and a black T-shirt, the words *Violent Femmes* splayed in silver across his chest. Briefly wondering about the nature of that band, she was shocked to see five students, mouths ajar, staring at her as if she'd worn her robe and slippers to school. "Is something the matter?"

Joey moved in closer, glanced around the library, and whispered, "Marianne asked you a question, but you've just been standing here for like six or seven minutes. You know, like ignoring her. We didn't know what to do." Joey's breath smelled of spearmint and cigarettes. Smacking his gum, he stepped back to join the others, like the final component of a Greek chorus preparing to utter a profound statement in unison. But there was only silence.

"Marianne," Maggie said, "why don't you come back after lunch and we'll talk about it then?" There. She'd barely missed a beat. Right? At the sound of the bell, Joey turned toward the door, the others following him without a word.

Later in the teacher's lounge, Maggie sat down with her spinach salad, adding grilled chicken and her special low-fat Catalina dressing. Claire Kincaid slammed the door to the microwave and walked over to join her.

"Well, did you bring pictures? How is Kellie doing? Is the baby adorable?" Claire asked. Maggie had noticed that since Claire had become a grandmother herself, she seemed overly anxious for everyone else to join her ranks. "I couldn't believe it when you called me yesterday. And such a short labor!"

Maggie stabbed a cherry tomato with her fork, uncertain how much to divulge. She was strangely drawn to this baby more than to anyone else, including Ross. The mysterious, immediate sense of attachment actually frightened her. How could she explain it to Claire? She swallowed the tomato. "No pictures yet. But yes, she is adorable."

Claire tore the plastic film off her Lean Cuisine Turkey Tenderloins with Stuffing. Although she appeared to be on a perpetual diet at school, she evidently lacked self-control at home. Maggie wished Claire would practice more willpower when it came to eating, but she would never hurt her best friend's feelings by harping on the subject.

"What is her name again?" Claire asked between bites.

"Julia Rose Fraser. Nice, don't you think?" Maggie pushed around a piece of grilled chicken.

"I love it," Claire exclaimed.

"I love her." It was out before Maggie could take it back.

"Well, of course you do, silly. Kellie has always been more daughter than step-daughter to you. And this granddaughter, biological or not, will be your own as well." Claire pushed the last bite of stuffing onto her spoon. "I can hardly wait to go shopping with you for pink dresses and those itty bitty socks with the rosebuds and lace trim. What color is her hair?"

"Kind of reddish blonde. And curly," replied Maggie, thankful she could answer such a simple question. But this was where the conversation needed to stop for now. "Going to the language arts curriculum meeting tomorrow?"

"Do I have a choice?" said Claire. "Besides, I wouldn't dare miss an opportunity for the 'powers that be' to tell us what ten new things we have to cram into our day next year. And I can't tell you how excited I feel about hearing the hottest theory on the best way to teach writing, all the while incorporating grammar in a natural and unstructured style. Oh yes, and how to get boys to enjoy poetry. God. Sometimes I wonder why I chose this subject. I'd really like everything to be more black-and-white, like math or library science. Want to switch jobs?"

This was nothing new. About two-thirds of the way through every school year, Claire pointed out how difficult it was to be an English teacher and how Maggie had it oh-so-much-easier since keeping track of library books entailed no gray area. Checking books in, checking books out, renewing them, repairing them, ordering new books, weeding old books, keeping books in perfect order so they could be found when someone needed them—it was all so logical. Maggie could go home at the end of the day without a stack of papers to grade and a list of parents to call. Little did Claire know her librarian friend, for the first time, was questioning the logic of everything in her life, including her job.

They cleared their containers off the table, glanced in the mirror over the sink to check for remnants of trapped food in their teeth, and left the sanctuary of the teachers' lounge.

Relieved to be temporarily free of Claire's questions, Maggie floated through the rest of the school day without incident.

Ross was already home when she walked in the house at 4:30, stirring the sauce for the lasagna they'd offered to take to Kellie's. Spencer sat patiently on the other side of the glass patio door, his gigantic paws covered in mud from the earlier showers that afternoon. He held his favorite red ball in his mouth—always ready, just in case Ross discovered a spare minute to throw it for him.

Acknowledging the obvious, Maggie attempted normal conversation. "Ross, dear, did you get off early today?"

"Glen and Elizabeth shoved me out the door, in spite of the clients who kept showing up with one more receipt they hoped to turn into a tax deduction. They thought I might want to get over to see my new baby granddaughter." Ross's enthusiasm over Julia had grown to the point of non-stop babbling. Maggie suspected his accounting partners had reached their limit with the proud grandpa for one day.

"Did you talk to Kellie? What time shall we leave?" Maggie wasn't entirely positive she would feel ready to go, no matter what the time.

"Let's go as soon as we put the dinner together," Ross answered. "Kellie's really having a hard time getting the baby to quiet down. She sounded pretty frazzled."

An hour and a half later, the hot lasagna sat in its carrier in the backseat of their station wagon. Maggie held the salad and garlic bread on her lap. She didn't know why she felt so nervous. This was her daughter and granddaughter she was about to visit. Any other new grandmother would consider herself fortunate to live only a couple of miles across town. The baby was healthy. Kellie would be a dedicated and attentive mother. Sean would try his best. In the driver's seat, Ross beamed like someone had just told him he could retire today and still have more money than he could count. Everything was perfect. Wasn't it?

Kellie stood waiting for them at the open front door. Relief washed over her face as Maggie and Ross carried the food into the kitchen. Either Kellie or Sean had already set the table, so Maggie poured the appropriate beverages—milk for Kellie and Ross, coffee for Sean, ice water for herself.

Ross looked around for a baby carrier. "Where is my precious dumpling?"

"Asleep in her room for the moment." Kellie frowned. "I don't expect it to last long the way it's been going. I just don't get it. She's nursing fine. I change her diaper constantly. What else could she possibly need?"

Sean sauntered into the kitchen, eyes bloodshot and drooping from lack of sleep. Silently he dished up the lasagna. Since none of them knew the answer to Kellie's question, they took their usual places at the table.

Forks halted in midair when the high-pitched cry came from the other room. Kellie wiped the corners of her mouth, sighed, and rose from her seat.

"I'll go." Maggie's tone told them there would be no discussion, so Kellie put her napkin back on her lap and passed the Parmesan. Ross took a sip of milk. Sean licked garlic butter from his thumb.

Ducks and daisies decorated all corners of the pale blue and yellow nursery, including the light switch cover. Assorted clothes, toys, and other infant paraphernalia were neatly stored in their designated places. Maggie turned on the dresser lamp. It quacked twice.

The crying turned to half-hearted whimpering and then stopped altogether.

Maggie undid the top button of the baby's perspiration-soaked sleeper as she carefully sat down with her in the rocking chair Ross had purchased a month before. Placing her cool hand on Julia's damp forehead, she whispered in her tiny ear, "I'm here now." Julia's body visibly relaxed as she turned her face toward Maggie's.

As if clutching a precious, unexpected gift, Maggie stroked her granddaughter's cheek. Hazily, she wondered if the others were still eating dinner. No matter. All remnants of her previous fear and uncertainty cleared neatly away.

Distant, hazy sounds traveled from the kitchen—possibly utensils clattering against empty plates. Then Ross's voice, unmistakably concerned. "Should we wait a minute longer or start cleaning up? Where is Maggie, anyway?"

Down the hall, in the blue and yellow nursery, Julia gripped Maggie's finger so securely, it tingled into numbness. Not daring to disrupt the soothing energy flowing from one to the other, they rocked and rocked, oblivious to the rest of the world.

Chapter 4

On Thursday of the next week, Ross left the office early once again, knowing the house would be empty. It seemed he couldn't concentrate on anything right now, and he was counting on some time alone. His usual efficiency had been put aside like a pair of practical shoes he knew he'd get back to sooner or later, when his feet hurt badly enough. Meanwhile, the tax returns piled up on the shelves behind his desk. Too many people these days just couldn't get it together before April 15, forcing him to file extensions. He'd managed to make a few necessary phone calls that morning but had given up when the first four clients didn't answer right away. He was losing patience waiting for the return calls. What was wrong with some people?

And the real question—what was wrong with Maggie?

He'd tried to ignore the way Maggie had acted the day after Julia was born, but the events of the last couple of weeks kept creeping into his mind. He couldn't quite put his finger on it, but something was different about her. And Maggie just didn't "do" different. One of the reasons he'd fallen in love with her after college, technically on graduation day, was her predictability. His own life up to that point had been troubling, beginning with his parents' divorce when he was seven. Surviving three moves in two years during junior high, Ross had then watched his older brothers leave home before he graduated from high school. Not to mention there had never seemed to be enough money. Ever. Somehow he'd managed to scrape together some cash, applied for every scholarship and grant he could find, and started college.

Marrying the first girl who looked interesting was, naturally, a big mistake. Laura, a cute but distressed history major, turned out to be an ill-fated match for Ross. The only positive thing to come out of that hopeless relationship was their daughter, Kellie. Besides having a long list of unfortunate personal issues, Laura wasn't exactly the mothering type, so Ross took over in the best way he knew how. By the time Kellie was two, Ross had divorced Laura, graduated from college, and bought a small house for him and his daughter.

Ross had met Maggie in the long lines of students waiting to be seated for the graduation ceremony, nurses lined up next to geologists, social workers beside musicians, and accountants alongside teachers. Barely twenty-one, Maggie had expedited her time in college by attending summer quarter every year. At first, she seemed exactly the opposite of Ross. She came from a traditional middle-class family, no dysfunction anywhere to be seen. The Taylors were hard-working, dedicated parents who provided endless possibilities for their beloved only child. They gave Maggie every ounce of their attention and encouragement, along with piano lessons, acne treatments, and a car at eighteen. Unfortunately, both Alex and Darla Taylor died in an automobile accident just eight months after Maggie married Ross. Her life plan securely in place, Maggie picked out a few sentimental keepsakes, sold the house she grew up in, and continued on her new journey with Ross and Kellie.

Ross thrived on Maggie's obsessive nature from the beginning. A place for everything and everything in its place was exactly what filled the vacuum in his life. He was convinced he could live with someone like Maggie forever. Smart, pretty, ambitious, and confident as to what fork to use during the third course of a fancy dinner party, she would be a wonderful mother to Kellie, supplying the family life he'd always dreamed of. From the moment they met, Ross could smell the oatmeal raisin cookies she'd bake for the school carnival, and feel the hand-sewn stockings she'd hang from the mantel at Christmas. Just the thought of what Maggie might bring his way was like a smooth touch of heaven. This time, Ross knew what he was doing.

After twenty-four years of marriage, everything had gone precisely according to Ross's plan. Consequently, even this slight variation in Maggie's behavior and routine thoroughly alarmed him. Not only did she refuse to tell him what had been bothering her the night of Julia's birth, she withdrew as if something horrible had happened instead of something wonderful. Although it had originally been Maggie's idea, she had seemed anxious about delivering dinner to Kellie's a few days later. Strangest of all, she disappeared into the baby's room for two hours that night, ignoring the rest of the family and never eating the very meal they'd prepared. Why didn't she bring Julia out to the kitchen with her to eat? Maggie loved lasagna, for God's sake!

Spencer trotted over to where Ross sat at the dining room table, his big brown eyes full of canine devotion, and laid his head on Ross's knee. At six months, the dog was already Ross's loyal buddy and confidant. A deep sigh escaped Ross as he scratched the front of Spencer's silky neck. He and Maggie had owned several pets over the course of their marriage, but this golden retriever was spoiling him for any other four-legged friend. Spencer's unconditional dedication and willingness to please made Ross appreciate him even more. Especially today.

"Do you think Maggie is going through some crazy midlife crisis or something?" Ross inquired of the dog. He knew she was perimenopausal—Maggie insisted they both use the correct terminology—but she assured him a daily twenty-five milligram soy supplement was all she needed. She had researched the pros and cons of prescription hormonal replacement therapy, deciding there were too many serious side effects. Why take a chance, she said, when menopause was a natural transition into just one more phase of a woman's life? Silly, she said, to make such a big deal out of it. After two hot flashes, one during the district librarians' quarterly meeting and the other a week later in line at the post office, she had picked up a bottle of soy capsules on her next trip to the pharmacy. A month later, the hot flashes went away, never to return, and the annoying emotional edge she often felt at the beginning of her period evened out quite nicely. Ross believed everything was under control. Obviously, a mistake.

"Surely she couldn't be having an affair." Having collapsed on the floor next to his empty food dish, Spencer jumped to attention at the sound of Ross's voice, cocking his right ear. "When would she work it in?"

Maggie accounted for every minute of every day, even the time she spent reading a book or watching a movie. It was all a part of her intricate plan, which normally worked so well for both of them. Maggie's skill at ultra-organizing her own life had gently nudged Ross into a routine of his own, something he'd craved right from the beginning of their relationship. Routine equaled security and stability. Besides, an affair would be completely out of Maggie's realm. It would be as bizarre as her impulsively deciding to splash in a mud puddle—it served no practical purpose, would be a source of complete regret afterward, and was far too messy. Maggie just wasn't the type to give in to a spontaneous moment of, well, anything.

"Maybe having a granddaughter makes her feel old. What do you think, my pretty boy?"

Spencer listened attentively, as if hoping to hear a familiar word like *ball, walk, car,* or *biscuit.* He nudged Ross's arm and received a pat on the head. Ross flopped over Spencer's silky ears to check their condition.

"Is that what you think it is, Spence? Maggie feels old? Now there's a definite possibility."

Spencer wagged his tail in agreement, shaking his ears back into place.

Just last year, when Ross turned forty-nine and Maggie forty-eight, they had given in to reading glasses. Like addicts, admitting they had a problem was half the battle. They could no longer see the newspaper over morning coffee, labels at the grocery store, or tell the cauliflower from the rice pilaf on their dinner plates.

At least with this particular issue, Maggie had accepted her fate, ordering blended bifocals, with a slight correction in the bottom half for reading and clear glass in the top half. She told Ross she wanted to wear them all the time instead of simply buying a drugstore pair she'd have to prop on the end of her nose. The glasses made her look sophisticated.

Ross, on the other hand, felt the frustration of a fifteen-year-old learning to drive a stick shift. He desperately wanted to see but didn't want to go through any hassle along the way. He impatiently fiddled with the over-the-counter glasses for three months, broke two pair, lost one, hated the whole process, and finally made an appointment to get contacts. Maggie shook her head when she found a dried-up lens on the back of the toilet tank the first week. She just glared at him, lips pursed, the morning he woke up and realized he'd fallen asleep without removing them. In silence, she wiped up the lens cleaner he dripped all over the bathroom counter every day. But Ross persevered until months later, when he finally became used to the contacts. No big deal, he announced.

But if that was it—if Maggie felt old becoming a grandma—then why wouldn't she leave the nursery the other night? Her behavior had been so out of character that evening, Ross had thought she might be sick or asleep in there. But when he peeked through the door, all he had seen was Maggie rocking Julia, eyes closed, totally peaceful. He didn't get it. One minute she seemed disturbed by their granddaughter's arrival, and the next minute happier than he'd ever seen her. Baffling.

They had both been looking forward to the baby's birth since the first day Kellie told them she was pregnant. Certainly, he and Maggie shared an exceptional life together. When all he could see were numbers and more numbers at the office, he knew he could come home to his adoring wife, his rose garden, and his joyful bundle of fur, Spencer. Plus, in spite of the inevitable aging process creeping in, he and Maggie enjoyed perfect health and looked forward to an active retirement. But secretly, not daring to mention it to Maggie, he yearned for an ounce of excitement, a bit of surprise, a new spark to their lives. Kellie's baby would be that spark.

Spencer whined at the sound of Maggie's car pulling into the garage. There must be something wrong, Ross thought. It was too early for her to come home. Usually she spent at least two hours after school getting the library back in order, preparing for the next day, making copies, conferring with teachers about their upcoming projects, or helping a student with research. School ended at 2:30, and it was only 3:05. This has been too much for her, Ross thought. Whatever the hell "this" was.

He met her at the back door. "Hi, honey. How was your day?" he prompted.

Radiant, Maggie's hazel eyes glistened; her face, slightly flushed, shone like dew on one of Ross's Brigadoon tea roses. He'd never seen her quite like this. It was a turn-on, actually, and he suddenly wondered if she might agree to a little afternoon nooky. Maybe this new version of Maggie would enjoy something out of the ordinary. The image of the two of them urgently ripping off each other's clothes and throwing themselves onto the perfectly made bed upstairs made him breathless in seconds. But why take the time to go to the bedroom? How about right here on the kitchen table?

"Hi, dear," she answered. "I had a terrific day. I thought I'd go over to visit Julia now. Want to come?"

Ross's daydream was cut short like a red Ferrari trapped underneath a Mack truck. It was still in motion, but the chances of it recovering its full potential were extremely slim. Groaning, he retrieved his coat from the back of the kitchen chair. He should talk to Kellie. She might have some insight as to her mother's mysterious transformation.

Chapter 5

Maggie sat perfectly still in the mauve living room chair next to the bamboo plant. School had only been out a week when it occurred to her she didn't have a clue what to do with her summer.

Certainly it wasn't unusual for most educators to be so overwhelmed at the end of the school year, they couldn't think past the final day. With semester exams, proms, and cruises on the lake, energy typically ran low. And when the final student walked out of the classroom, teachers remained. There were grades to finish up, reports to file with the district office, materials to sort through for next year, and furniture to move out of the way so the maintenance crew could clean and paint over the break. Maggie, clearly more satisfied in her comfortable library than a classroom, nevertheless had non-fiction inventory to finish, a missing and lost book list to print, purchase orders to turn in to the school bookkeeper, and damaged books to send off to the bindery. A few staff members mentioned immediate trips to Maui or Puerto Vallarta, but most collapsed for a week or so, catching up on sleep and families.

Maggie was considering giving up her self-imposed, stringent routine in which every minute of each day was accounted for.

From September to mid-June, her week began with the 10:00 Sunday service at the Summerhill Presbyterian Church, and then grocery shopping and composing a list of school projects for the week ahead. A healthy dinner complete with a homemade low-calorie dessert—usually her special oatmeal cookies or low-fat apple crisp—topped off the agenda. Each weekday, after finishing up at school, she had things to do and places to go. On Mondays, Wednesdays, and Fridays, she drove to the all-women's circuit training gym, only seven blocks from home, for a forty-minute workout. On Tuesdays and Thursdays, she scheduled appointments or stopped by the library for a new book. Smart, complicated mysteries were her preference—those that challenged her problem-solving skills right up to the last page. Saturdays were saved for cleaning every inch of the house, followed by a bubble bath around 4:30, dinner out, and maybe a movie in the theater. Video rentals were for Friday nights.

Since Maggie did almost all the cooking, Ross washed while Maggie dried the dishes every night. Weather permitting, Ross would then head outside to fuss with one procedure or another to his rose bushes, and Maggie, while either organizing laundry, folding laundry, or ironing, would call Kellie to hash over the day's events. If they could work it in, Maggie and Ross enjoyed watching *Jeopardy* together at 7:00. Each had a current book on their nightstand waiting, but at 9:30 it was lights out.

Sex wasn't quite as frequent as when they were younger, but for two people in their forties, twice a week seemed just about right. Ross reported that the guys at the office complained they were lucky to get it twice a month anymore. Maggie knew a healthy sex life was part of the glue that held them together; plus, it boasted the added benefit of a clear complexion.

Normally Maggie's summertime schedule included tackling home projects, such as painting the bathroom, redoing the recipe file, or sorting through items to donate to the Lakeside Abused

Women's Center. However, circumstances had been nowhere near normal since the day Kellie had given birth. Julia Rose Fraser was pulling and tugging the rug out from under her grandmother's safe, systematic haven.

At first, Maggie told herself it was because she hadn't known Kellie as a baby. Ross came into Maggie's life when Kellie was barely two, and Maggie had bypassed the days of diapers, bottles, colic, first words, first steps. But from the moment Maggie and Ross met, Kellie had gratefully accepted Maggie as her mother. Their bond was immediate and secure, transcending even the moods and minor rebellions of adolescence. And now, Kellie had a daughter of her own.

Sweet baby Julia, strawberry blonde hair frizzing up around a perfect heart-shaped face, had managed to disrupt Maggie's comfort zone. Julia presented a new, demanding world, a reason for existence. Indeed, this in itself was not unusual. Many grandparents felt exactly the same way. But if she dared look deeper, Maggie knew it was definitely more remarkable than a woman bonding with her granddaughter. Plus, the dream of the two young girls she'd had the night of Julia's birth only added to her bewilderment. Maggie, who appreciated and actually relied upon the tangible, proven aspects of life, could not make sense of what was happening to her. It was nonsensical. It was uncomfortable. It was just plain weird.

She really needed to stop thinking about it.

Grateful for the distraction of the ringing telephone, Maggie pushed her current thoughts to the area of her brain reserved for needless worrying and unattainable crossword puzzle solutions. She straightened the wrinkled armchair cover she'd been unconsciously fidgeting with, and reached for the phone.

"Hey, stranger. I miss you already!" It was Claire.

"Hey there, yourself. What's up?" Maggie feared her distracted behavior that spring might have led Claire to the conclusion she was losing her friend either to hormones gone astray or a form of mental illness not yet identified.

"Do you feel like taking a short walk down by the lake?"

"Sure, why not?" Since she hadn't really begun her usual summer routine—in fact, could barely focus enough to remember what that routine might actually entail—Maggie felt a rare sense of freedom in choosing to do something unplanned. "Meet you at the picnic area off Cedar Road?"

Clearly surprised Maggie was willing to go, Claire said, "Terrific. See you there in about thirty minutes."

Maggie wrote a note for Ross, made sure Spencer's and Cleo's water bowls were filled, grabbed her sunglasses and sunscreen, and tied a light sweater over her shoulders. Cleo halted her midday primping, meowed as if being unjustly deserted, and then happily claimed the patch of sun on Maggie's chair. Spencer's big eyes drooped in disappointment as he realized he wasn't invited.

In the car, Maggie recalled when she and Ross, newly married, had envisioned their ideal place to live. Almost in unison, they described a small town within an hour of a busy city, plenty of trees and mountains, friendly people, and without question, a beautiful lake nearby. As it happened, shortly after their conversation, they drove through Summerhill on an excursion to Canada, a trip they had hoped would help them unwind following the loss of Maggie's parents. Built around Lake William, the town of Summerhill appeared just as they had pictured, with the bonus of Seattle only forty-five minutes away.

A few weeks after Ross and Maggie made the move from California, Claire approached Maggie at an evening literature course and asked if she wanted to join her at the local Dairy Queen after class. A friendship as true and effortless as their vanilla cones began that night.

Once, in those early years, Claire called Maggie up, sobbing into the phone as if her mother had died. As it turned out, she had. Claire's mother was a petite gray-haired woman with the same weakness for ice cream as her daughter. A car accident had killed Patricia as well as the other driver, a thirty-six-year-old recently divorced man who'd downed one too many martinis at the Blue Ox Bar. A kind policeman had come to Claire's home to tell her the shocking news. Evidently, the accident had happened just two blocks from the mini-mart on Pine Avenue; the officer said there was a pint of Ben and Jerry's Chunky Monkey in the front seat. Maggie drove straight over to comfort her friend with a willing shoulder, a fresh box of tissues, and a bottle of chardonnay. Late into the night they discussed how they now shared one more experience—the death of parents in a car accident.

"It takes a while to get over," Maggie cautioned her friend.

And when Kellie, a first grader with pigtails and her two front permanent teeth barely showing, fell off the top bar of the jungle gym at recess and broke her arm, it was Claire who showed up at the hospital minutes after Maggie. The two friends hugged and cried, all the while repeating, "She'll be fine. It could've been so much worse."

Now Claire was waiting, a floppy lime green sun hat shading her face. Maggie pulled into one of five parking spaces, turned off the ignition, and immediately felt better. The clear water of the lake, glistening with what Kellie had called "sun sparkles" as a little girl, provided a welcome reprieve from the confusion she'd been feeling lately.

The two women started up the hiking path, barely visible this time of year with wildflowers covering every inch of the hillside. The aroma resembled a delicious, well-seasoned gourmet dish. Anyone could attempt to distinguish the pine and fir from the wild rose and honeysuckle, but why bother when the end result was blended perfection? The women walked perhaps a mile with barely a word, and then stopped in a clearing where the blue water spread out ahead for miles. They sat on a makeshift bench constructed from stumps and scrap lumber. Maggie regretted not bringing Spencer along. He would've gone crazy sniffing and racing all around.

"I like your new haircut. It really brings out your eyes," she said to Claire. "I'm thinking of doing something different with my hair too."

Claire was speechless. Maggie rarely noticed Claire's changes in hairstyle, and absolutely never considered changing her own. Next she might suggest something totally bizarre, like getting her nails done.

"Maybe I'll go for a manicure next week," Maggie continued. "Ann Sutherland, from the math department, recommended a girl she really likes."

Claire pretended to adjust her hat while gradually regaining her composure. She changed the subject. "Did you hear Josh Dickinson was accepted to Harvard?"

"No, but I'm not surprised," answered Maggie. "He's a genius and happens to be a nice kid, as well. I wonder if his parents had something to do with it, or if he just arrived on the planet that way."

"Who knows? Most of the time I think kids turn out the way they're going to turn out no matter what we do. I've finally quit beating myself up about the infinite ways I could've been a better parent. Kathleen and Ben are so unlike each other, and we raised them just the same. This nature-versus-nurture premise is silly. Babies come ready-made with an entire set of interests and talents and personality quirks." Claire's children had grown up into independent, wonderful adults; but there were times, especially during their teenage years, when she had almost given up on them. "Jack and I just shake our heads sometimes and wonder why we worried so much. Looking back, it seems like they managed on their own while we just stood helplessly by."

"You're probably right. But the structured librarian in me wants to believe there's more to it than that."

Claire fixed her shoelace and continued with more gossip. "And what about Bill Guthrie?"

"What about him?"

"He's getting a divorce, giving up teaching—two years before full retirement—and moving to New Orleans to live in that heat and humidity. Can you believe that? I don't know what got into him."

"Maybe something happened to him that he couldn't ignore." Maggie suddenly felt strangely close to Bill, a science teacher to whom she seldom spoke. He attended every staff meeting but was noticeably too preoccupied with his own thoughts to participate much.

"Maybe," Claire said. "I guess he's always loved jazz and wants to find somewhere to play his saxophone all day and night. Oh, well. They'll find some new young teacher to take his place."

They sat silently, as Maggie speculated on what might have happened to Bill Guthrie. A religious experience? A midlife crisis? An unusual incident with a new grandchild?

Maggie looked at her closest friend and decided to take a chance. "Claire?"

"Hmm?"

"May I talk to you about something?" Maggie couldn't believe what she was about to say.

"Of course. What? What is it?"

Claire's blatant look of anticipation struck Maggie as rather comical. She imagined Claire wondering if she suffered from a life-threatening illness, or was having a relationship with a man she met at the drugstore and was planning to leave Ross and run away to France. It would be just like Claire to dream up a wild story. She suspected Claire's heart was thumping like the hind leg of a dog getting his belly scratched.

Claire grasped Maggie's hand and looked into her eyes, waiting.

Maggie compelled herself to go on. "It's not anything you're probably thinking. But it is quite out of the ordinary, at least for me. And you have to promise not to repeat this to anyone. Do you promise?"

Claire hesitated for a split second. "All right, all right. I won't tell anyone. Just spill it."

"I think I've known Julia for a long time."

"Julia? Well, how could that be? She's only three months old!"

Maggie sighed. "I don't know how it could be." The pressure on her hand tightened to the point of escalating pain, and she slowly eased her fingers from Claire's grip.

Claire stood and paced in front of the bench. She stooped to pick up a half-empty bag of discarded bread but abruptly straightened again, empty handed. "This definitely isn't what I thought you were going to say, Maggie. I'm not exactly sure what you are telling me. Why should feeling close to Julia bother you?"

Maggie could see she'd left Claire somewhere in between shock and disappointment. She decided to proceed cautiously. "Well, she is extraordinarily familiar to me. Not just comfortable. Familiar. You can't be familiar with someone unless you already know them, can you?"

Claire sat again, leaning back on the bench. Her hands started to shake. "I don't know. When you put it like that, then yes. I mean no. Geez, I don't know what I mean, Maggie. It just doesn't make sense."

"You don't know how much I agree with you. What I am certain of, as odd as it may sound, is she knows me and I know her. We are at home with each other even more than you and me or Kellie and me or Ross and me." Now frantic and hysterical, Maggie suddenly shouted, "My head hurts. My stomach is in a constant knot. I break out in a sweat thinking about being with Julia, yet when I am, I'm terrified to let her go. I don't know how to tell any of this to Ross. I can't explain it. I don't know why I'm like this, I just am. And, Claire, it's driving me fucking insane!"

Claire stared at Maggie as if they'd both been hit by a school bus. In all their years of friendship, Maggie knew Claire had never heard her use anything close to the f-word. Obviously her confession was more than Claire could handle. She was positively speechless.

A moment later, though, she found her voice, pitched in the range of a squeaky hinge in need of a squirt of WD-40. She looked straight into Maggie's eyes and wailed, "Sweetheart, do you think you're one of those psychic medium type of thingamajigs?"

Maggie paled. She and Claire looked at each other as if for the first time all afternoon. Then the laughing began—the kind of loud, intense, uncontrollable laughing that would cause some women to wet their pants and not even care. Instead, these two friends—Maggie, her precise, organized, predictable world gone desperately awry, and Claire, baffled and stunned beyond belief—laughed until tears ran liberating and free.

Claire dug around in the back pocket of her shorts and handed Maggie a tissue. "Here," she said. "It's still folded, so I'm pretty sure I haven't used it."

They sniffled and laughed again. Neither one could think of anything more to say.

Totally exhausted now, the women started back down the trail. Maggie spotted something floating in the water below and grabbed the bag of bread Claire had almost picked up earlier. At the bottom of the hill, Claire headed toward the parking lot, but Maggie stopped.

"I'm not quite ready to go yet. I'll see you later."

"Sure," said Claire. She didn't question her about anything else, no doubt aware that it might take some time for their previous conversation to sink in. Hugging Maggie, she whispered, "Everything is going to be all right."

"I hope so."

Maggie waited on the shore until the duck she had seen from the hillside swam toward her. It was a fairly young female, brown and dowdy, paddling round and round in circles, as if performing for an audience. Maggie broke off chunks of the stale bread and threw them into the water. When she'd eaten her fill, the duck splashed her wings, squawked directly at Maggie, and glided away. Although it really didn't suit the drab-looking bird, Maggie felt obliged to call it Daisy.

That night Ross wrapped potatoes and corn in foil, made a salad, and barbequed two appetizing salmon fillets. Maggie was happy to let him take charge. They ate out on the patio, Spencer at their feet waiting for just a tiny morsel to drop from the table. When none did, he gave up and stepped into his blue plastic wading pool. A big slurpy drink and a cool soak in the water apparently hit the spot almost as much as a bite of salmon.

"You're kind of quiet, Mag. How was your visit with Claire?"

"Oh, it was nice. Great to catch up."

Ross waited, but since Maggie didn't add anything else, he said, "I think I'll mow the lawn. It's supposed to rain tomorrow. Would you mind cleaning up by yourself tonight?"

"Not at all, honey. The dinner was delicious, by the way."

Maggie actually preferred cleaning up alone once in a while. Ross did a good enough job, but he never thought about washing out the coffee pot or cleaning the sink or wiping off the stove or sweeping the kitchen floor. She grabbed a clean dish towel and got to work.

At 8:15 when Maggie walked upstairs, Ross was still mowing, Spencer following him along every row with a ball in his mouth. She decided to get organized for the summer by composing a to-do list for the rest of the week. It would be a start anyway. As she retrieved her pad of paper and pen from her desk, the telephone rang, startling her just enough that she banged her knee on the sharp edge of the open drawer.

Claire sounded serious on the other end. "Maggie?"

"Hi. Is everything okay?"

A momentary silence and then, "Well, yes and no."

Uh-oh, Maggie thought. "What is it?"

"I just want to tell you that what you said today about knowing Julia for a long time ... Well, I have someone ... uh, there's someone I feel the same way about. You know, like we've met each other before."

"Really?" *Wow*, thought Maggie. *What a shock.*

"Yes, really. So I don't believe you're crazy or anything. I thought telling you this might make us both feel better."

"Well, thanks, Claire. I guess it does." Maggie realized she probably wasn't going to learn anything further.

"Another thing, Maggie."

"Yes?" Maybe there would be more after all.

"You know I don't go to church very often, so this may sound like an unusual request. But I do believe in God and all, so … Well, anyway, you go to church every Sunday, and maybe you're already doing it, but could you pray about this?" Claire's rambling finally came to its point.

Maggie smiled. "I'll pray for both of us." They hung up, promising to take another walk by the lake soon.

Well, what an interesting day this has been. No longer in the mood to write her list, she vowed to do it promptly in the morning. She laid her paper and pen in her underwear drawer next to her mother's diamond engagement ring. If she died before Ross, he and Kellie knew they would find all of her meaningful belongings right there.

She could see Ross bagging up the grass clippings on the side of the house. He'd have to throw the ball for Spencer a few times and refill his wading pool. Maggie estimated it would be a full thirty minutes before he'd come in. She turned her gaze toward the dusky summer sky. It was almost the solstice and wouldn't be dark until after 9:00, but she still found the moon. First quarter tonight, which meant it would be full, bright, and beautiful in seven or eight days. The thought of it made her tremble with anticipation. A full moon might bring another fascinating dream.

She could hardly wait.

Chapter 6

When school started in the fall, Maggie was acutely aware of the curious looks from her colleagues, as well as students who'd known her before. The superficial changes were few but obvious, considering Maggie hadn't changed anything about herself in years. She had bravely let her hair grow out over the summer, allowing her stunned hairdresser to touch it up with a few reddish highlights, and spent an extra minute or two each morning feathering it out here and there. The tips of her fingers glimmered with burgundy polish, showing off her new Celtic ring with its repetitious loops and symbols. It was a relief for some to see she still wore her basic outfit of calf-length skirts and sweater sets, although their loose, flowing style exhibited a new attitude.

Maggie MacKenzie had come to life. And no one knew what to make of it.

As usual, she had come into her library a couple of weeks before school started to prepare for the first day with students. Shocked to see how stark and bare the room looked, she couldn't believe she'd allowed its plain appearance. She immediately drove to The Learning Center, where she purchased posters of prolific authors, classic books, and research tips. When the massive room still didn't seem right, she returned to pick up a hanging mobile of the Dewey Decimal System, a bulletin board kit with the theme "Fall into Reading," and a life-sized cardboard cutout of Mark Twain. Six potted plants completed the new look for Summerhill High School's media center. It had never been so festive.

By the end of September, Joey, the bold young man who had woken Maggie out of her stupor the year before, had become one of the library regulars. He, too, revealed a new haircut—basically the chopped-up, wild, tousled style popular with his crowd. A small gold hoop decorated one ear, and Maggie was tempted to reach out for it as she'd done a thousand times on the merry-go-round as a child. On a bright October day, orange leaves swirling outside the library windows, Joey lingered after fourth period to ask a question.

"Mrs. MacKenzie, why is the moon so cool?"

Maggie stepped out from the biography aisle. "Well, not everybody finds it—uh, cool, Joey. Why do you think you do?"

"I can't figure it out. The rest of the universe is, you know, interesting and all, but there is just nothin' more fascinating than the moon." He looked down at his black skate shoes, significantly worn at each big toe. "My girlfriend thinks I'm crazy."

"Do you find yourself getting up in the middle of the night to look at the moon?" Maggie blurted out.

Joey looked like someone had discovered the stash of *Penthouse* magazines hidden under his bed. "How did you guess that?" he whispered.

"Now you know something about me too." She put her hand on Joey's shoulder and walked him to the door. "I can't explain it either."

She suspected they had more to discuss about this topic, but Claire's arrival made Joey dart down the hall.

"Ready for lunch?" asked Claire.

While Maggie retrieved her room key from her purse, Claire stood in the doorway plainly admiring both her friend and the spruced-up library. Claire's classroom had always been packed with zillions of visuals, all pertaining to grammar, literature, famous authors, the five-paragraph essay, and iambic pentameter. Kids in her classroom were given so much to look at, they occasionally found it difficult to pay attention, Maggie had kindly pointed out to her once. But Claire said she couldn't stand the thought of giving anything up. What if the one poster she took down conveyed an idea that would bring some reluctant reader to a fascinating book or a struggling writer to be more confident about his ideas? Then what kind of teacher would she be? Claire had demanded.

They made their way down the hall amid slamming lockers, squealing girls, and strutting football players. Maggie turned toward her friend. "How do you think I can reach Bill Guthrie?"

Claire halted in front of the door to the teachers' lounge. "Why would you want to do that?"

"If I recall, he used to do a pretty neat unit concerning lunar phases and human behavior. A student approached me about the general topic, so I thought I'd see if he would send me his materials."

"Oh," said Claire. "It's, uh … funny. I got a, uh … postcard from him a couple weeks ago. It has his address and phone number." She stifled a nervous laugh.

"Really?" Maggie looked hard at her. "Have you been in touch with him then?"

"I haven't responded to his card, if that's what you mean."

"Well, what did he say exactly?"

Claire waited until Don Henderson and the two surly girls he was escorting to the office passed by. She stepped directly in front of Maggie. "Only one sentence. 'I'm sorry I didn't get to say good-bye.'"

They remained face to face for a moment, and finally walked in to get their lunches.

After school, Maggie stopped at the gym for her Wednesday workout. She went through the motions of the familiar machines and jogging stations, but while she was contracting her inner thighs, her mind was elsewhere. Luckily, she didn't see anyone she recognized, so she finished the forty-minute circuit, stretched out afterward, and left without talking to a soul. At home, Spencer greeted her with a mouthful of toys, grunting, whining, and wiggling all the while. Cleo lay stretched out on the back deck, the autumn sun warming her feline bones. She didn't bother to look up.

Maggie poured herself a glass of cool water from the refrigerator's dispenser before sitting down with the phone. She had debated all afternoon whether or not to call Bill Guthrie, wondering if Claire would mind. But then, why should she? Maggie might have been imagining Claire was acting oddly when she asked about Bill. There was only one way to find out. She dialed the number Claire had given her.

Bill answered on the fifth ring.

"Hi, Bill, this is Maggie MacKenzie."

"Maggie? It's marvelous to hear a familiar voice!" Bill sounded simultaneously disappointed and relieved it was Maggie. "How are you?"

Maggie hesitated a mere second before saying, "Well, fine, I guess. School's going well, and I'm a grandmother now, you know."

"Yes, I remember your daughter had a baby. Last spring, wasn't it? That's great."

"How about you, Bill? Are you doing okay?"

"Sure."

Maggie waited. When he said nothing more, she decided to get right to the point. "Say, Bill, remember the unit you used to do about the effects of the moon on human behavior? Do you think you could send me the materials?"

"Why, certainly, Maggie. I don't really have any use for them now. Do you want to use them in your library?" Bill sounded surprised that she might be daring to go outside her comfort zone with this subject.

"They're for a student." She paused again, and then added, "I guess for me too."

"No problem. I'll dig them out and send them to you at school."

They both were silent. Maggie didn't know what to say next, but she didn't want to hang up. Apparently, Bill didn't either.

"So, what are you doing to keep busy, Bill? Playing any music?" She thought she'd better ask. Claire would undoubtedly quiz her about the details of their conversation.

"As a matter of fact, I play in a jazz quartet. Just four nights a week at a local hotel lounge, nothing fancy. It's something I've always wanted to do." He let that sit a minute. "How's your friend Claire?"

"Just the same. Spending too much time stressing over her students. She's the one who gave me your number. I didn't realize you were friends with her outside of school."

"Well, we weren't actually." His voice was barely audible.

"Oh?"

As if he'd been waiting all these months to confess to anyone who would listen, he announced, "Maggie, she was the reason I got a divorce and left Summerhill."

"What?" Maggie felt like someone had bumped the remote and she'd accidentally landed on a rerun of *The Twilight Zone*. "I thought you said you didn't know her outside of school."

The floodgates opened. Everything Bill apparently had wanted to say to Claire for years, he now told Maggie. "I felt a fondness for Claire from the moment I met her. I never told her. I never acted upon it. I was married, for God's sake. Claire was married. But I liked her so much. I thought about her all the time. It wasn't right, so I started avoiding her."

Relieved Bill couldn't see the shocked look on her face, Maggie wondered how she could not have noticed any of this.

There was no stopping him now. "I can't explain it, Maggie, but it was like I'd always known her. I didn't know how to handle it. I still loved my wife, but it wasn't fair to her. I wasn't a good husband to her anymore. So I left."

Always known her. Was that what he said? Maggie came close to dropping the phone. "And how do you feel now?"

Bill sighed, cleared his throat, and then sighed again. "I tell myself I've done the only thing I could have. For my wife, for Claire, for me. I have a nice life here in New Orleans. But, Maggie?"

"Yes?"

"I still think about her every minute of every day. It's like an essential part of me is connected to Claire and I don't know why."

Hundreds of miles across the country, Maggie's jaw dropped as she realized Bill's secret was also her own. She started to tell him just that but stopped herself. Not the right time.

"Bill?"

"So? You think I'm out of my mind?"

"Amazingly, no. Not at all. I just think you need to tell Claire what you've told me. You won't regret it." She hoped she wasn't setting Claire up for disaster.

"I don't know if I can. She has no idea I feel this way."

"I think you'll be surprised. Trust me on this, Bill."

They said good-bye and hung up just as Ross pulled in. Maggie prayed she'd remembered to defrost something for dinner.

Reverend Chamberlain was talking about the wheel within a wheel from the Book of Ezekiel when Maggie decided she should confess to Claire about calling Bill Guthrie. She hadn't felt ready to mention it all week at school, mainly because of the many questions floating around in her head. Should she tell her everything? Should she say they'd only talked about the moon unit? What should she say regarding how Bill was doing? Here in church, next to her darling Ross, stained glass surrounding her, it became clear. She should encourage Claire to make her own phone call to Bill and let the natural consequences come about. After all, Bill had sent a card to Claire and given her his phone number.

For the first time in her life, Maggie speculated who else might be dealing with a secret. Take Fred and Darlene Kramer across the aisle, for instance. She'd been acquainted with them for the entire twenty-three years she and Ross had been attending Summerhill Presbyterian, but knew nothing more about them than that Fred was a meter reader for the gas company and Darlene liked to relax with a fun Janet Evanovich novel after a long day styling hair at the New You Salon. Tuning out Reverend Chamberlain's sermon, she imagined the undisclosed events lurking within the Kramer household. Was Fred hiding a drinking problem? Did Darlene fantasize about the hunky cop, Joe Morelli, in those novels she read? Was their marriage as content as it looked to the rest of the congregation, or was it all a pretense until their kids graduated from college? Did Fred and Darlene feel like they'd already known each other when they met?

Maggie's parents had brought her up in a church just like Summerhill Presbyterian. She never questioned the beliefs presented to her as the absolute truth. Certainly her parents' religious values were not to be challenged. And since Ross hadn't experienced the stability of any church growing up, he'd welcomed Maggie's religion as his own. It wasn't a topic worthy of discussion, really. The two of them always felt completely at home, first with Reverend Thompson, and then later with the younger, more modern version, Reverend Chamberlain. Kellie had loved the Sunday school as a young girl, and Maggie was sure she planned to bring Julia when she was old enough.

But lately uncertainty clouded up around Maggie like a morning fog that refused to burn off. She questioned every minuscule aspect of life, including the religious beliefs that had always guided her. Deep in the pit of her being, in the very place most people seldom visited, Maggie doubted whether she could truthfully continue practicing any form of Christianity until she figured out precisely what was going on between Julia and her. It was possible the feelings she had for Julia had nothing to do with God or the Presbyterian Church. Maybe they were just human emotions, completely detached from anything of a spiritual nature. But that was the part Maggie couldn't quite get past. The whole experience felt more spiritual than the hundreds of Sundays she'd spent listening and singing on a wooden pew.

She closed her eyes and prayed for resolution on the issue, just as she had done many times since Claire's request.

On Monday, a student office aide delivered a package to Maggie from Bill Guthrie. Good old Bill. Always trying to accommodate people, he hadn't forgotten the initial reason for Maggie's phone call.

Maggie walked down to Claire's room at 2:45. The majority of students had already zoomed away from the parking lot, and those who remained in the building were most likely at the Halloween dance committee meeting. She found her friend hunched over her desk, a pile of papers—some handwritten, some typed—stacked next to her like a mound of laundry multiplying with every glance.

"Hey," Maggie said.

Claire peered over her reading glasses. "Oh, hi. Did I ever tell you how smart you were to give up language arts for the library? These essays are about to kill me."

"Yes, I think you've mentioned it a time or two." Maggie loved this woman. "Can you take a break for a minute?"

"Why not?" Claire pulled off her glasses, rubbed her right eye, and patted the chair next to her, usually reserved for discussing grades with her students.

Maggie approached Claire's desk but decided to stand. "I called Bill Guthrie the other day."

"You did? Why?"

"Remember, I told you about the materials for a student? You gave me his number."

"Oh, right, right. Well, what did he say?" Claire had the same uneasy expression as when she'd come clean to Maggie about receiving Bill's postcard.

"You need to call him, Claire."

"Oh, I couldn't do that. I shouldn't. Why would I?"

"Just call him." Maggie refused to let her friend get out of this one. "Don't you want to?"

"Why would I want to?" Claire's eyes were getting bigger and bigger. "What would Jack say?"

Maggie stepped closer. "Jack doesn't have anything to do with this. You need to get on the phone and give Bill a call. For yourself."

Claire picked up her purple pen and grabbed another essay from the pile.

"Believe me. I know what I'm talking about. Call him." Maggie headed for the door, an astonished Claire still holding the purple pen in midair, like a divining rod in search of water.

Chapter 7

"Do ye think anyone will miss us?"

"Me da's had too many pints to know if he's missin' me or not."

"Ay, me da too. And me mam be snorin' like a wood saw next to me brothers."

Two girls run hand in hand down the hillside to the water. The dark-haired one leads the way, pulling the other girl toward the rocky bank.

"'Tis the loch, Gillian?" asks the red-headed girl.

"Ay. Lovely, ain't it?"

"Lovely but freezin'." The girl shivers. The top button is missing from her wool sweater. She tugs her scarf tighter over her red hair. Pulls her hands up into the sweater. The wool smells damp and musty. "'Tis only the start o' February. We must be daft to be out here at night."

Chunks of ice float on the water. So cold. Black darkness. They huddle together on a flat boulder at the shore's edge.

"Just wait," says the dark-haired girl. "I know it be your first night here visitin', Rebeca, but ye willna regret comin' with me."

Ripples in the water. Splashes. A duck swims nearby.

"Here she comes," whispers Gillian.

Brown duck, splashing, quacking. The dark-haired girl digs around in her pocket. Tosses oats in the water. "Sorry, that be all I have for ye tonight, me love."

The duck gobbles the oats. Swims round and round in a circle. Looks up at the girls.

"She be right friendly, Gillian, just like ye said. Ye kept her alive all winter, didna ye?" Locks of red hair blow in the cold wind.

"Ay, Rebeca, I suppose I have."

Moonlight shines through mist on the mountains as they climb up the hill. "Do ye have a name for her? She be needin' a grand name."

They stop in the narrow path. White shows underneath one edge of dry, shriveled brown heather. They look closer at tiny petals. A spot of yellow.

"'Tis a sign o' hope an' survival, ye know, for spring and all," Gillian says. "We need a bit o' hope on this wintry night. Let her name be Daisy then."

They see the cottage ahead. Chimney smoke curls upward. Endless stars and the gigantic crescent moon shine brilliantly in the black sky.

"Daisy, sweet Daisy!" the girls call over and over. They chase each other up the hillside, laughing, laughing.

Maggie jerked herself awake and bolted straight up, the covers held tight to her chin. Ross was already climbing out of his side of the bed. He approached her cautiously, not sure if she was still asleep, and put his hand on her shoulder.

"Maggie, honey? You were calling out—something about a flower. Did you have a nightmare?"

Tears streamed down Maggie's cheeks. Terrified and shaking, she tried to answer him, but comprehensible speech lurked as distant as the dried heather in the dream. Finally, she managed to say, "I don't know, Ross. I don't know what it could be."

"Tell me what the dream was about."

As restless clouds swirled around every side of the full moon out their window, Maggie clung to Ross as if he were her lifeline to reality. "It's not *what* the dream was about that scares me. It's *who* it was about!"

Chapter 8

On her daughter's first birthday, Kellie rose at 6:00, a full hour before Julia's usual waking time. She sat down with her coffee and newspaper and looked over the list she'd made a few days earlier. Maggie had trained her as a young girl in the invaluable ritual of list making. "Kellie, sweetheart," she had said, "if you make a list, you get all those thoughts about the tasks you have to do right out of your head. Then they don't seem overwhelming. You can concentrate on one thing at a time, and before you know it, you will have everything all checked off. Won't that feel magnificent?" Well, yes, Kellie admitted as she got older. It did feel magnificent. She made a conscious effort, however, never to become as compulsive with lists as her mother, who was known to add something she'd already accomplished just so she could immediately cross it off.

But on this important day, like the dedicated daughter she was, Kellie made a list.

1. Groceries: lettuce, mushrooms, eggs, lemons, chicken breasts, rice, powdered sugar, milk

2. Bake lemon cake
3. Pick up balloons
4. Deposit Sean's paycheck
5. Remind Sean about birthday dinner
6. Iron tablecloth
7. Mop kitchen floor
8. Talk to Mom about Julia

Every item would be a snap, all completed before she knew it, except number eight. Kellie dreaded the talk with her mother, although it was long overdue. Her dad had begged her to talk to Maggie a few weeks after Julia was born, but Kellie had ignored his pleas. Surely he must have been imagining things. Initially Kellie was unwilling to admit a change had come over her mother almost at the exact time Julia was born—a startling change that was most likely an indication of more changes to come. Every day she waited for Maggie to return to what they all thought was her normal, predictable, obsessive, yet wonderful self. But it just hadn't happened. And now an entire year had passed. She simply couldn't stand it any longer.

Kellie rarely saw her biological mother. It wasn't that they weren't on amicable terms; it was more like they weren't on any terms. Kellie had long ago accepted that Laura was not going to be a mother to her. She might call Kellie once in a while or even come to visit her every couple of years, but the feeling between them was more like that of a distant aunt and niece—yes, they were related, but it was all right with both of them if that was as far as it went. When Kellie allowed herself to think about it for more than ten minutes at a time, she started to feel abandoned and alone. It was her own mother, after all. If her dad had not remarried, it might have been a definite reason for therapy later on.

But not only did he remarry, he married Maggie. Maggie, with her sense of responsibility easing her into the role of stepmother. Maggie, with her immediate and genuine love for the girl who was the offspring of her beloved Ross. Maggie, who knew the importance of reading story after story until Kellie had them all memorized; baking cupcakes for the third grade Christmas party; answering endless questions about where the stars came from; sewing costumes for the seventh grade production of *The Wizard of Oz*; and taking Kellie shopping for her first formal dress, although she did not care for the boy taking her daughter to the dance. When her friends asked Kellie about her "real" mother, she described Maggie. Maggie, who had always been there for her and was now turning into a stranger.

This was something Kellie just didn't need right now. It was exhausting being a new mother. Trying to take a shower was a major event. Some days she never did get one. She had hoped to leave her job as a travel agent, stay home with Julia, and find some sort of work when Julia started kindergarten. She should have known it was only wishful thinking. Sean tried to justify his occasional unemployment by pointing out that his sporadic work as a roofer brought in excellent money when the jobs did come around. And there was the inevitable conversation about how much better it would be if he quit working for someone else and started his own business.

But nothing ever changed, the bills piled up in between jobs, and Kellie arranged to continue working at home. Confirming flights, typing up promotional letters, and checking on lost luggage usually took a mere three hours a day—easily accomplished while Julia was napping or entertaining herself with her toys. She missed the face-to-face contact with excited clients planning a vacation, but Kellie knew this part-time work kept her foot in the door of the employment world, just in case she decided to abandon Sean altogether. Calling it quits with her marriage was always in the back of her mind, but since Julia's arrival, she didn't dare entertain that thought for too long.

Oh, it was true she was considering having sex with the cute new guy from the office. She'd heard her girlfriends confess to their own affairs, and she always swore she'd never be so stupid.

But when he'd dropped by to pick up the United tickets for Dorothy Rafferty's trip to Florida last September, they had talked and laughed for a good hour, keenly aware of the tiny smiles for no reason, the flirting eyes, the jokes. Tempting, very tempting.

Kellie was positive, however, she needed to talk about what was going on with her mother and baby daughter. She picked up the phone to ask Maggie if she and her dad could come over a few minutes early for dinner.

In the car, Maggie smoothed the front of her navy slacks and looked at the birthday present she held for Julia, one of those toddler chime balls with a yellow duck in the middle. Other gifts sat in the backseat of the Subaru—two adorable outfits, chunky picture books, and a soft, cuddly doll. Those would be fun. But for some reason, she suspected Julia would go directly for the chime ball.

She glanced admiringly over at Ross, still handsome in middle age, with barely ten gray hairs. Everyone had wondered if their marriage would work. They didn't say it right to their faces, but their silence made it clear. She had surprised even herself by marrying someone who didn't share her idyllic upbringing. And on top of everything else, he had a daughter, for heaven's sake! But there seemed to be no genuine choice at all—when she agreed to marry Ross, Maggie couldn't deny the deep sense of knowing it was the only thing to do. Ross would be her partner in life no matter what anyone thought was right or wrong, sensible or senseless. It was one of the few times in her life she moved forward without planning every detail, calculating the risks, or analyzing the situation to death. In fact, it was the only time she could remember willingly relinquishing control of her life.

Until now. This past year had filled Maggie with complete joy and utter frustration all at once. And she found it impossible to explain it to those around her when she didn't understand it herself.

53

As Ross knocked on Kellie's door, it opened on its own. Indecipherable, harsh-sounding words came from the back bedroom. *Uh-oh. Sean and Kellie at it again.* Maggie looked at Ross; they simultaneously frowned and walked in.

From her plum-colored bean bag chair in the living room, Julia grinned and squealed at the sight of her grandparents. But it was Maggie she toddled toward, holding both hands up.

"There's my sweetheart!" Maggie held her close, kissing the delicate part of her neck right below her ear lobe. A smell of fresh laundry and baby lotion enveloped the birthday girl.

Kellie appeared, hugged her parents, and sat on the edge of the tapestry-covered ottoman. "The dinner will be ready soon, but can you sit down for a minute? I need to talk to you both about something."

Ross chuckled. "Sounds like we've reversed roles here. Isn't that what we used to say to you whenever you didn't do your best at school or came home late? Are you going to ground us?"

"Very funny. No, you're not grounded. But there is something going on that all of us have been afraid to talk about. It involves you, Dad, but it's really about Mom and Julia."

"Yeah," Sean said from the kitchen doorway.

"I think I know what you're getting at," Ross said, "but how does that issue involve me?"

"Because you've been ignoring it lately just like I've been doing, and it's not going away."

Sean, looking relieved to discuss any topic not pointed directly at him, added, "Things just aren't the same as they used to be in this family."

Maggie bristled, shifting Julia to her left knee. "And what exactly is the problem?" *This could be interesting.*

Ross, Kellie, and Sean looked from one to another uncomfortably before turning to Maggie. Maggie sat expressionless, but Julia raised her arms as if to say, "Come on, let's hear it!"

Sean finally began. "You've been driving us all crazy."

"Really?" Maggie wondered if they had any clue how crazy she'd been driving herself.

"Yes, you have," Ross jumped in. "You're totally consumed with Julia, and speaking for myself, I'm feeling ignored and neglected. I don't know what to expect from you anymore, Mag." Exasperated, he added, "You're just not the same."

Maggie put Julia in the playpen, where she promptly pulled herself up and peered over the top edge. The Raggedy Ann doll, stuffed elephant, and plastic blocks, all of which had probably captured her full attention an hour earlier, sat abandoned at her feet. Totally absorbed in the situation, she watched the adults, as if waiting to see what would happen next.

Doing her best to stay calm, Maggie wondered what her daughter, who had initiated this intervention, had to say. "Kellie?"

Kellie squirmed in her chair. She stood up and paced in front of the others. She opened her mouth, closed it, and finally sat down next to Maggie. "It seems to me that there are two issues here, Mom."

"Is that so? Can you be specific?" Even under pressure, Maggie appreciated a person's ability to clarify the concerns at hand.

"Well, one, you are giving Julia all your attention and the rest of us feel left out. And two, your personality is changing in the process. We're worried about you."

Ross and Sean, relieved Kellie had taken over, nodded enthusiastically in agreement.

Maggie didn't know whether to be angry or amused. "I see."

Kellie took a deep breath and went on. "I guess I'm kind of jealous. I didn't get to have this attention from you when I was a baby. And some days I feel like Julia loves you more than she loves me. And she's only a year old. What's it going to be like when she gets older?"

Sean looked at Maggie. "Yeah."

"I just want to know if you have some kind of explanation for the change in you, Maggie," Ross said. "Are you feeling all right?

Is there a problem you'd like me to help you with? What is the reason for this new you?"

"What is the 'new me' exactly?"

They all started in at once, but Ross won out. "Well, for twenty-five years you've taken care of the ironing on Wednesday nights. Now I see you hanging up clothes right out of the dryer and running that hand steamer thing over them. And usually it's just the night before you want to wear something! Why? Next, we always have scalloped potatoes with our meatloaf, but last month you fixed that spiral pasta stuff with the weird powdered cheese. Don't you like scalloped potatoes anymore?"

Kellie interrupted. "Mom, you used to fill your gas tank up before it dropped down to the halfway mark, but last week you actually ran out of gas and had to call me to come and get you. And what about your fingernails? Short with clear polish. You've never done anything else to them. Plain and simple, and they've always looked nice. But now you're going to a manicurist? Look at them today—silver, with a gold crescent moon on each one. I can't believe it!" Her voice hit a shrill note, like a tomcat facing his rival.

Evidently tired of standing, Julia sat down inside the mesh playpen, engrossed in the scene before her. She looked over at her grandmother.

"Sean? Do you have anything to add?" Maggie asked, grateful to be the one asking a question.

He sat for a minute with his head down and then finally looked up. "Yeah, I guess I do. I never thought I'd say this, but I miss the Maggie who used to come in and immediately straighten all the pictures and lampshades. Look at that picture over there. Don't you want to straighten it?" Everyone turned their attention to the slightly lopsided print of pastel water lilies. On a roll, Sean leaned forward. "Where is the mother-in-law who cared about me enough to point out that a decent haircut might improve my chances of getting a better job? Huh? Where is she now? Don't you care about me like you used to?"

The silence hung heavy, like a wet sheet waiting for the breeze to pick up and finish drying it.

"My turn?"

Everyone in the room looked at Maggie and waited, afraid to officially give her the go-ahead.

Struggling to maintain her composure, Maggie began. "Ross, honey, do your shirts look okay? Any wrinkles?"

Ross hesitated. "Well, they're fine, I guess."

"And what did you think of the new pasta dish I fixed last Tuesday?"

"It was quite tasty, actually."

"Kellie, sweetheart, have you ever run out of gas and had to call me or your father to come and help you out?"

"I suppose a few times over the years, yes."

"And what really bothers you about my manicure?"

Kellie peered down at her hands. "I wish I could afford to get mine done like yours. They're classy."

Maggie started to relax as she felt her sense of control returning. "Sean, dear, do you truly feel like I don't care about you anymore? Tell the truth now."

Sean looked like one of Maggie's students who had to think of a quick excuse for a torn book cover. "Well, deep down I know you'll always care about me. At least as long as I'm married to Kellie."

"All right then," said Maggie. "I think we've narrowed the problem down to this—I've changed slightly and it's hard to get used to change."

"That's probably true, Mom," said Kellie. "It wouldn't be that big of a deal if it was someone else making these changes, but this is you we're talking about. We just weren't prepared for you to change in any way. Ever."

Ross wasn't satisfied. "But why is this happening? Is it Julia? Is it a midlife thing? Are you happy or unhappy? Why?"

Maggie smiled at him. Oh Ross, the man of her life. The man who liked dependable structure even more than she did. She

57

should've known he would need further explanation. But could she tell him what he wanted to hear?

"I'm not sure I know what's going on exactly," she started, her voice cracking. "I only know that when Julia was born, my life was altered in a way I didn't expect. It's indescribable, really. But it doesn't mean I love any of you less. I'm sorry if you've felt neglected. I will definitely work on that."

"That's it? That's all you can say?" Kellie asked.

"I've told your father about some strange dreams I've been having." Gulping down the lump in her throat, she added, "The two girls in the dreams are sort of familiar, but I'm not sure who they are or why I'm dreaming about them. It's frustrating to me. And confusing. I suppose I look at the world a bit differently now because of all of this."

Maggie let that sink in for a minute. This was as far as she was willing to go. At least they had aired their concerns. Maybe they could live with her "remodel," as long as they knew there was nothing life threatening going on.

Leaving the others with their thoughts, Maggie picked up Julia and took her out on the deck. Kellie could put dinner on the table without her. The early spring sun was hazy and too far away to send them much warmth. Maggie spotted a robin on the peeling deck rail as she sat on the wicker chair, grabbed the frayed blue and lavender plaid blanket that Kellie kept there, and wrapped it around them. Much better. Julia's wild reddish hair formed a soft pillow between the back of her head and her grandmother's chest. What *was* happening to her? Tears welled in her eyes, but she had no idea if they came from joy or sadness.

Neither she nor the robin noticed the corners of Julia's mouth turn up ever so slightly, a distant wisdom blazing deep behind her blue eyes. She snuggled in closer to her grandmother. For the moment, the secret would stay contained inside the little girl celebrating her first birthday with a chicken dinner, lemon cake, and the four adults who loved her.

The robin flew away without a glance in their direction.

Chapter 9

One Sunday morning the next winter, Kellie let herself in her parents' front door. Although Sean had begged off going to church again, Ross had put the pressure on Kellie to come along anyway. Lately, Sean was going his own way and Kellie was going hers. Remarkably, they each seemed happier with this arrangement.

Kellie propped Julia up in the corner of the sofa, her Strawberry Shortcake overalls bunching up around her legs. Certainly there had never been a cuter toddler. She had contentedly settled into a routine of sleeping, eating, playing, and being loved by Kellie and Sean. But whenever her grandma Maggie, or "Gammy" as she now called her, appeared, her eyes lit up like two glittering candles, and cries of pure delight could be heard practically across the street. It was a scene the rest of the family was still trying to figure out.

Julia's second Christmas had been incredible. Even Sean got into the shopping mode. Baby dolls, pink jeans, stuffed dogs and cats, lamb's wool comforters, and picture books were lavished upon her. Julia's pleasure, however, didn't seem to be so much in receiving the gifts, but in seeing how happily everyone acted while giving them to her. She put her family in a terrific mood.

As Kellie reached to remove Julia's mittens, Cleo immediately appeared from nowhere, purring loudly in their faces. Amused, Julia permitted the cat to pat her lap in a futile attempt to make a nest.

"Anybody home?" Kellie called out.

Ross came down the stairs dressed in the gray slacks and maroon cable-knit sweater Kellie and Sean had bought him for his birthday two weeks before. His thinning dark hair was still damp from the shower. Kellie was surprised to see Maggie right behind him in her unmistakable non-church attire of jeans and a sweatshirt.

"Hi, honey," Maggie said, making a point to hug Kellie first and Julia second. Cleo abandoned Julia's lap, shaking her head in disgust as she landed in the middle of the living room floor.

"Everything okay, Mom?" asked Kellie, still startled by her casual outfit.

Ross answered for her. "Your mother wants to skip church today and spend some time with Julia." He and Kellie exchanged a look of mutual exasperation and inevitability. This still happened more often than they were comfortable with.

"Well, I guess that's all right," Kellie said. "What are you going to do?"

Maggie turned toward her daughter. "I thought we'd look around at the mall. After that, I'm not really sure. But don't worry. I'll have her back by noon or one, in time for her nap."

"Guess it's just you and me then, Dad. Better get going." Kellie kissed Julia on the top of her head. "Be good for Grandma."

"Mmm, Gammy." Julia beamed, a thin string of drool escaping her lips.

And so it was, on this icy morning, that Maggie and her beloved granddaughter went off by themselves. The traditional family roles had changed significantly since Julia's arrival, and Maggie knew Ross and Kellie would benefit from some time to themselves. Kellie seemed to have something on her mind lately, and her father was just the one to hear her out.

These days Maggie tried not to focus on the mystery of the extraordinary bond she shared with Julia. The dreams she had at night, however, were impossible to ignore. They scared her to death yet comforted her at the same time. She'd scrutinized every detail so many times that any meaning had been lost in the process. Then why, she wondered daily, couldn't she quite let go and forget about them? She longed for someone—a complete stranger off the street would do—who could offer any type of reasonable explanation.

The mall parking lot was full as Julia and Maggie pulled up in front of the J. C. Penney entrance. Julia bantered happily as Maggie scooped her out of her car seat, adjusted the hood on her snowsuit, and removed the collapsible stroller from the rear of the car. Julia settled in, turning her head only to confirm Maggie's presence behind her. At the end of every parking row was an enormous pile of plowed snow, making it almost impossible for Maggie to see the oncoming cars. Once inside the store, they scurried off to look at clothes for Julia. Maggie held up a white cotton dress with tiny violets trailing down the bodice. Julia stood up in her stroller, both arms reaching out for it.

"Pitty, Gammy, pitty!"

At the checkout stand, Maggie paid for the dress and put the package in the back storage pouch of the stroller before wheeling Julia over to the food court. She ordered a peach Julius for herself, with a second small cup for Julia, and sat down at a table to figure out how to spend the rest of the morning. Three girls Maggie recognized from school sat across the way, sodas and an assortment of Taco Bell containers covering their table. She smiled at them but knew she should go no further. The kids she ran into around town were unpredictable. They either came running up to her to say hi, or their body language made it clear it would definitely not be cool for them to acknowledge her in any manner. For some, socializing with a teacher at the mall would result in complete humiliation. Maggie had learned to stand back and let the teenagers do whatever they needed to do. She didn't take it personally.

Just as she bent down to undo the stroller's seatbelt and lift Julia to her lap, she heard a deep voice mumble, "Mrs. MacKenzie?"

Startled at first, Maggie saw it was only Joey Martinez. "Oh, hi there, Joey. How is your weekend going?"

"Pretty good." Joey, looking faintly distraught, acted as if there was more he wanted to say, but he didn't know how to get it out.

"Something on your mind, Joey?"

"Umm ... sort of. I guess I saw you sitting here and wondered if I could ask you a question."

"About school? A problem with your senior project?" Maggie studied the young man's face. He looked as worried as Spencer when, as a puppy, he didn't know for certain if what he'd just done was going to receive a "good dog" or a "bad dog." "What is it, Joey?"

He pulled a chair over from another table, noisily scraping the tile floor all the way. Sarah Kaufman, one of the girls Maggie had smiled at earlier, glanced admiringly at the dark and mystifying Joey. Julia looked him over and clapped her hands twice. Joey smiled awkwardly, apparently confused as to why the school librarian had a baby with her. But he didn't ask. He gazed at his large brown hands, picked at a scab on one knuckle, sighed, and then sat up straight and faced Maggie.

"Mrs. M., have you ever seen yourself in the moon?"

"Pardon me?"

"Like when you look at the moon—you told me you look at it all the time—you know, well, when you look at it, what do you see exactly? 'Cause I see myself. Not my face, not like the man in the moon that some people see, you know, but like inside myself. The real me. The me I don't even know about sometimes. Like what I am now and what I'll be down the road, you know, my future and everything. It's as if the moon and me, we have this relationship and it knows everything about me. If I concentrate on it, everything I've been wondering about seems so clear—what I should do about certain stuff, like what to say to my girlfriend so she'll like me better, or what I should write my English paper on to get a good grade, or that I should check the air in my tires because one of them is low. It's spooky, Mrs. MacKenzie, and I don't know if it's real or if I'm just making too much of it. Do you think I could be dreaming? And it's the most powerful, this feeling or communication or whatever it is, during the full moon. Shit, it's gettin' so freaky, I hate to see the sun go down. But I can't help myself. I've gotta look for it every night." Suddenly he clamped his jaw shut hard, like the basset hound on the old Nestlé chocolate commercial.

They sat in silence for a minute. More like a full five minutes, actually. Maggie had realized what her response was going to be about halfway through Joey's apprehensive, rambling statement, but she wanted to give herself a chance to find the right words. He'd made a very personal confession, which, she imagined, had taken more courage than probably anything he'd ever done. He deserved a serious, heartfelt answer. Oh God, the pressure. The first words out of her mouth might determine something critical for this boy.

"Joey, thank you for telling me. This universal connection you've described actually helps me figure out something about myself."

"Really? What exactly?" He stopped. "Uh, if you don't mind me asking, Mrs. MacKenzie."

Maggie hesitated for a moment. "No, I don't mind. You've been very honest with me." She wondered if Joey was as fearful as she of what might come next. "I've had a couple of unusual dreams. During the full moon. Dreams I can't seem to figure out or forget."

"Whoa! No kidding. During the full moon?" Joey leaned forward and started fiddling with the plastic keys on Julia's stroller.

Julia patted his hand and said, "Nice."

"Granddaughter?" Joey asked Maggie.

"Yes." Maggie took a deep breath. "Unlike you, Joey, I look forward to nights with a full moon. But these dreams are extremely real to me, and I don't know quite what to make of them."

"Man oh man. What we're gettin' into here goes way beyond that packet of stuff you got from Mr. Guthrie. I didn't see anything in there about a direct hookup with the moon or a librarian's spooky dreams. Mrs. MacKenzie, I don't want to pry or anything, but can you tell me what they're about? If it's not too personal, you know." His left eyebrow raised itself unnaturally high.

For one brief, intense moment, Maggie considered telling Joey every detail of her dreams. Lord knows, she had them memorized and could easily relay the specifics. But should she? Joey was a student. She didn't feel right crossing the invisible line a teacher worked hard to maintain—letting her students get to know her well enough to like and trust her, yet keeping certain aspects private in order to maintain a level of untouchable respect. She shouldn't tell him, at least not right now.

"I appreciate your wanting to help, Joey, but I think the underlying feeling, the emotion of the dreams is what's important, don't you? You've made me realize how the dreams allow me to feel uniquely connected to the rest of the world. Or to the universe, you could say. How about you?"

He looked right at her and said, "I feel great. Really great. It's like the moon gives me power to do anything in my life."

"Well, then, maybe you and I should just try to accept what's happening as something positive. We don't necessarily need to understand it." The profound, sensible thoughts formed in Maggie's head just seconds before the words spilled out of her mouth. Instead of questioning their source, she welcomed them gratefully.

"But why? Why is this happening to me?" Joey asked. "Nobody else I know, well, besides you, has anything bizarre going on with the moon. At least, they don't talk about it if they do." He glanced shyly at Julia as she spooned a bite of peach slush out of her small cup. "Oh, well. I'd better go." Joey stood up. "Thanks for talking to me, Mrs. MacKenzie. See you tomorrow at school."

"Anytime, Joey. I don't know why this is happening either, but maybe we'll figure it out as we go. You are a very insightful young man." Maggie smiled as Joey sauntered away.

She began clearing the table, only to find Joey standing right in front of her once more. "Sorry I said 'shit' earlier, Mrs. MacKenzie."

Maggie coughed to head off the laughter in her throat. "No problem, Joey. Sometimes it just fits."

The frost on the streets had given way to shiny, wet pavement; the sun, although low on the horizon, shone brilliantly against the patches of lifting fog and pale blue sky. Ice crystals on the Douglas fir trees dripped and sparkled. This postcard-like backdrop, along with the talk she'd had with Joey, directed Maggie to the place where she and Julia would spend their remaining time together. Exhilarated, she pointed the car toward Lake William. From her seat, Julia could only see the back of her grandmother's head, but still captured the essence of what she was feeling. In unison, they both sighed and smiled.

The beautiful day had brought out people of all ages, from an elderly woman sunning herself on the bench facing Hemlock Bay, to the four towheaded boys, definitely related, chasing one another with broken branches. Everyone wore thick coats and scarves, along with ruddy cheeks and dripping noses. Maggie wheeled Julia along the sidewalk leading down to the same area where she'd stopped two summers ago following her spontaneous admission to Claire. The vision of the startled look on Claire's face still made her giggle.

"Gammy funny," Julia said, giggling too.

Maggie felt a slight regret at not confiding in Joey more than she had. But how could she explain what she didn't completely understand herself, especially to an eighteen-year-old? She squatted down in front of Julia, always an attentive listener.

"Julia, what do you think about your crazy grandmother?" Julia looked up at the sound of her name and grinned, showing all eight of her teeth. "I can't talk about any of this to your mommy or your grandpa. They would flip out. I tried to talk to Claire, but now she's all wrapped up in her own weird experience. You don't think I'm off my rocker, do you? You still love me just the same, don't you?"

"Lub Gammy! Kiss Gammy!" Julia shrieked. Maggie leaned over for a slobbery kiss.

"Do you think it's a case of overactive hormones? I'm at that age, you know. My estrogen level is dwindling; my egg basket is almost empty. Lots of women feel differently during these years. And the moon can definitely play a part in our emotions, just like Joey said. It's all quite normal."

"Umm, moon," whispered Julia.

"I thought my life was just fine before you came along, Julia Rose. But now I see there's so much more. I feel like I've been missing something all this time and didn't realize it. I just don't know what to think of the dreams I've had. Maybe I read a similar story in a book once. But who are those girls? Why do they seem so real? Why can't I stop thinking about them after all these months?"

Julia had stopped listening, her attention drawn to the water behind Maggie. She was slightly frantic, and Maggie fumbled to pick her up. "What is it, sweetheart?"

"Day? See?" Julia pointed toward the lake, her short legs pushing to free herself from Maggie's arms. "Day! See!"

Maggie took her hand and carefully led Julia down to the cold shoreline, wet sand kicking up behind them with each step. A stray piece of blackish green seaweed landed on a rock and slid down to rest next to Maggie's boot. Then she saw the duck, fifty yards or more out in the water, regarding them intently. *She must be hungry,* Maggie thought. "Oh, honey, it's only a duck. Just like the lamp in your bedroom. Can you say duck?"

"Day see," said Julia matter-of-factly, correcting Maggie like a patient wife would do for her husband who had mispronounced something. "Day see, Gammy, day see."

"Day see? What is day see?" For a minute Maggie tried to convince herself Kellie had taught Julia a song or read her a story with some words she had now mixed up, but saying it out loud forced her to admit what she suspected was true. She examined Julia's bright face, her wise eyes, her red hair glistening in the January sunlight. And Julia returned her gaze.

Trembling, Maggie fell to her knees next to her granddaughter. *Oh my god,* she thought. *How could she possibly know?*

"Daisy," they shouted together, as the duck fluttered up above the water and skimmed out toward the gleaming depths of the lake.

Chapter 10

Four nights later, after watching a rerun of *The Waltons*, Maggie turned to Ross in bed and kissed him tenderly. The old Maggie would never have initiated sex, but the new one had no problem with it whatsoever. Ross, always a willing participant, was excited by his wife's newfound assertiveness. It was one change in her he seemed to readily accept. But while he promptly fell asleep afterward, Maggie lay wide awake.

Claire would say insomnia was characteristic of any fifty-something woman, along with night sweats, moodiness, and sporadic periods. However, Maggie knew the problem was something different—unidentifiable, really—and although she had taken a long time to rule this out, she knew it was definitely not hormones or lack thereof. The fact that she was able to eliminate a single piece of this complicated puzzle was comforting.

Was she insane? It would almost be a relief, something tangible, to consult a psychiatrist, to have every friend and family member try to help her sort it all out—the dreams, the feelings, the duck, Julia. It would be liberating, Maggie thought, to assign any reason to it all.

It was peculiar how she so easily accepted a new order of expectations and priorities these days. Surprising events, both during the daytime hours as well as at night, were becoming more and more commonplace, and thereby, a fresh definition of normalcy to Maggie.

Wrapping her sky blue terry robe around her, but leaving her feet bare, she made herself cozy in Ross's worn-out recliner near the bedroom window. She opened the window an inch or so, letting in the still brisk but marvelously refreshing air, sitting motionless and praying once again for an explanation to all her feelings. Ross breathed heavily across the room, as thin, wispy clouds passed over the moon like strands of angel hair cotton over a solid gold Christmas ball. Maggie swore she felt someone smooth the hair away from her temple.

"Listen to me," says the girl with the dark hair. "Try puttin' both legs over the bog's edge at the same time, Rebeca."

The red-headed girl tucks her long locks into a blue wool cap she takes from her pocket, pulls her skirt up to her knees, and then jumps down with both legs together. "There!"

They run downhill, side by side, the full moon lighting their path just enough to keep them from falling. Frozen lake is black and glossy. Two ducks skim toward them in the shallow, melted pool near the shore. "'Tis our Daisy, and she's brought a friend out tonight on Loch Leven," shouts Gillian.

Chunk of bread for the ducks, chunk for themselves. Back and forth until the bread is gone. Harsh cold. Hands back in pockets.

"Ay, Gillian, me legs are shiverin' like a shorn sheep in the winter!"

The dark-haired girl nods. Snow starts falling. The girls scurry to a shepherd's lean-to. "Even so, can't bring meself to go back to the house right now. Can ye, Rebeca?"

"No, no, the men be gettin' downright unruly with the liquor in 'em. 'Though they might be all sleepin' by now. Let's stay here just a while longer, Gilli."

"Ay. I heard your men folks talkin' about leavin' in the morn. Didna your da say ye'd be goin'? Couldna ye find a way to stay?"

Rebeca is quiet. And then she says, "I heard 'em too. But I want to stay a wee bit longer, no matter what he says. Gillian, will ye speak with your mam?"

"Certain I will. She'll listen to me."

Snow falls silent and heavy. The girls huddle closer under the shelter. Stillness and silence all around them. Warmer now. Content. Suddenly a scream. A piercing explosion. More screams.

The girls stand up, unsure which way to go—toward the house, or away.

"Rebeca?"

"What?"

"Guess 'tis time for me to know your other name."

Rebeca looks up the hill, afraid. "Campbell, it be. Rebeca Campbell. And yours?"

Gillian stands, reaching for her companion's hand. "Maclain. I'm a Maclain, o' Clan MacDonald."

They run through deep snow. Toward the house. Daisy and Loch Leven behind them.

Part 2

*The most beautiful experience we can have
is the mysterious.*

—Albert Einstein

Chapter 11

It could have been a Norman Rockwell painting. The sun shone cheerfully on freshly swept sidewalks, warming the assortment of dogs decked out with Uncle Sam hats and bandanas tied around their necks. All children small enough to fit in strollers were happily awakening from their morning naps, seizing on the excitement of the popcorn-munching crowd. Big-footed clowns, some on tiny comical bicycles, made amusing faces as they tossed bubble gum and Tootsie Rolls. Six blocks away, Lake William shimmered, as if anticipating the boats, water skiers, and laughter that would bring it alive later in the day. The sky was cloudless and vibrantly blue. It was already a memorable Fourth of July for five-year-old Julia.

Maggie, Kellie, and Julia had arrived early to get a spot near the middle of the parade route. Just two months away from starting kindergarten, Julia swung her legs back and forth from the edge of her own child-sized lawn chair, waving the flag Ross had bought her for her first parade. The three ribbons tying back her ponytail—red, white, and blue, of course—still formed a perfect bow; and somehow, in spite of all her fidgeting, her white sneakers remained white. Jumping from Maggie's lap to Kellie's, constantly peering down the street, Julia emitted a contagious joy that allowed Maggie to forget her worries and relax.

The last few months had been the most difficult Maggie could remember for Kellie. She had finally gathered up the nerve to leave Sean, a step that in Maggie's mind had been inevitable. Quickly trading in her at-home travel agent work for full-time newspaper advertising, she took advantage of every opportunity for advancement with the small but respectable *Summerhill Chronicle*. Maggie supported her, even when Kellie had told her about the affair she'd had, and admitted she'd been riding the roller coaster of Sean's never-ending vision of success far too long. Oh, her poor loving and tenderhearted daughter. Her romantic dreams were shattered.

"How's Sean doing?" Maggie asked while Julia waved to a clown bearing candy in his canvas bag. "Is he working?"

"Oh, off and on, like usual. It's sad, you know. He's imagined hundreds of terrific ideas for businesses, but he just doesn't quite know how to turn them into reality." Kellie rubbed sunscreen on her arms. "I think he might actually be getting close to giving up and just trying to find something steady with the city."

Maggie looked over the top of Julia's head toward Kellie. "Would you—"

Kellie interrupted her before she could finish the obvious question. "No, I wouldn't consider going back to him. Not now. Too much has happened."

To hide her relief, Maggie bent over to help Julia get the wrapper off the Tootsie Roll she'd picked up from the curb. For weeks, Maggie had been listening to Kellie fret over how to tell Julia that Sean would always be her father, although he didn't live with them anymore; that none of their problems were her fault; that Mommy and Daddy still cared for each other but not in the way married people should; that their love for her would never change; and so on.

"Say, how did the conversation about you-know-what go with a certain someone?" Maggie tipped her head toward Julia.

"Mom, you won't believe what happened," said Kellie.

Maggie straightened her spine in preparation.

Kellie lowered her voice. "I started in with the speech I'd practiced with you a million times, but Julia stopped me right away. She said, 'Mommy, I know how you must feel. But it's not your fault.'"

"Really?" Confused, Maggie asked, "Isn't that what you were going to say to her?"

"It gets better. She told me that sometimes things happen we can't control. She said later in our lives we will understand why events occur the way they did, and that all our experiences lead to who we're supposed to become." Kellie stopped to take a breath.

"You're making this up. She used those words?"

"Well, not exactly in complete sentences, but that's what she meant. And she gave me an example."

"You're kidding."

"No, I'm not. She said when her goldfish died, she blamed herself for not giving it enough attention or remembering to feed it. But then she realized—she actually said this—that the goldfish had come into her life to teach her an important lesson. As if the fish had a choice in the matter."

"I'm stunned. Did she say what she supposedly learned from the goldfish?"

"Oh yes."

"And?"

"Well, to quote Julia directly, 'Mommy, nothing really dies. It stays with us in our remembory. Or in the lesson it teached us. Don't you see?'"

"I'll be damned," said Maggie. "She never ceases to amaze me. Wait until I tell your father."

"Why didn't Dad come with us today?" Kellie asked.

"I couldn't budge him. He said he wasn't really thrilled with parades in the first place, and besides, he wanted to weed and water his roses before it got too hot."

Kellie frowned. "He keeps everything in your yard gorgeous, Mom, but I could never stand all the dirt, bugs, and sore knees. To me, it's a waste of a beautiful morning."

"I agree completely." Maggie brushed a bee from her forehead. "He promised to fire up the barbeque later, though. Of course, he can't wait to listen to Julia's version of all the excitement. And he'll come with us to see the fireworks over the lake tonight."

"Oh, I know." Kellie pulled Julia away from the street and back to her chair.

Actually, Maggie hadn't pressed Ross, since she enjoyed time alone with just her girls. As often was the case when daughters became mothers, Maggie and Kellie had grown closer since Julia's birth. Kellie in particular seemed to appreciate Maggie more, perhaps realizing how difficult it must have been for Maggie to acquire instant motherhood status when she married Ross.

Kellie tossed Julia's empty popcorn bag into a nearby garbage bin. "How's Claire doing?" she asked Maggie. "Have you seen her much this summer?"

"Unfortunately, no. I guess we've both been busy," said Maggie. "Although that's no excuse really."

A gold Mustang convertible carrying the mayor crept toward them. Up for reelection in November, Betty Sternberg gave a royal wave that was as perfect as her approval-seeking smile.

"Gammy, when will the horses be coming? You said there would be horses," Julia said.

"I think I see some way down the street, sweetheart. They'll be here before you know it."

The Summerhill Cement truck roared by, a huge American flag hanging from its side, followed by gymnasts performing handstands and back flips all the way down the street. Maggie waved at a few familiar faces from school.

"Gammy! Mommy! Get up, get up!" Julia frantically pulled both of them to their feet and over to the curb.

Neither Maggie nor Kellie could see what she was so concerned about. They looked at each other over the top of Julia's head, perplexed.

"Julia, what is it?" Kellie asked.

But Julia wasn't talking. She stood, left hand at her side, gripping her miniature flag. Her right hand covered her heart.

"What is she doing?" asked Maggie.

"I have no idea." Kellie edged Maggie closer to the curb so they could look down the street. Even through their sunglasses, the dazzling sun prevented them from seeing anything other than the cars and floats and high school band heading their way. Surely there was nothing out of the ordinary.

"Do you hear them?" Julia asked, without looking up.

"Hear what, honey?" Maggie lowered her face next to Julia's, attempting to see and hear from her perspective.

Julia whispered into her grandmother's ear. "Pipers. The pipers are coming."

Pipers? What? Maggie looked down the street one more time, finally spotting a man in a tall, fuzzy hat behind a gigantic banner. Beyond him, towering pipes fanned out like reeds on a pond of green plaid. She straightened up and turned to Kellie. "It's only bagpipes. Probably the Scottish band from Seattle."

Kellie looked confused. "How would she know …?"

The unmistakably haunting resonance of drums and bagpipes overwhelmed them, as the group of twelve men and three women passed in front of them playing "Scotland, the Brave." One white-haired gentleman, hairy knees exposed between his high socks and kilt, looked directly at Julia and winked. But Julia remained steadfast, hand over her heart. It was so unlike her not to smile and wave at the man, Maggie thought, but what stunned her were the tears she saw in Julia's blue eyes.

"Mom, why are you crying?" Kellie asked.

"Me?"

"Yes, you."

Maggie dabbed at her face with her fingers. She couldn't believe it. Why would she be crying? Julia turned to her and reached for her grandmother's hand. Neither one said a word. Kellie openly stared at them.

The rest of the parade was insignificant compared to whatever had just happened. Even the Red Hot Mamas, the Idaho group of middle-aged women with their shopping carts, outrageous hats, and hysterical antics, failed to entertain the three of them. Kellie suggested Julia might be tired, and they should consider beating the crowd out of the downtown area. Clearly relieved, Maggie agreed. It was only 12:15 when they picked up their chairs and headed toward Locust Avenue to find the car.

Kellie clicked the latch of her seatbelt and put the key in the ignition. Julia sat peacefully in the backseat, looking out the window, her flag resting on the seat beside her.

"Mom, has Julia ever seen or heard bagpipers when she's been with you or Dad?"

"Never." Maggie adjusted the air conditioning and turned off the radio, hoping to calm her racing mind. "I'm sure of it."

"Well, I know she hasn't with me or Sean, or on television either. I just don't understand how she knew about them in the first place, not to mention her unusual reaction." Kellie turned left onto Spruce Avenue. She held her foot over the brake pedal as a squirrel ran across the road.

About six blocks from the house, Maggie realized Ross would be checking the time, wondering when to start the barbeque later. He'd have everything organized and would become frustrated if the day's schedule was thrown off in any way. What would she and Kellie tell him about the parade? What would Julia tell him?

"This is truly mind-boggling," continued Kellie. "Where could this have come from?"

"It's from before," Julia stated matter-of-factly.

Maggie and Kellie, having forgotten Julia was even in the car with them, were startled by the small voice from the backseat. Maggie's jaw dropped. Kellie raised an eyebrow.

"What do you mean, sweetie?" Kellie asked, glancing in the rearview mirror at her daughter.

Maggie turned toward the backseat. "When was it?"

Julia's face seemed as childlike as the summer afternoon when, as a toddler, she first splashed her feet in delight at the edge of Lake William. Yet her answer to Maggie's question revealed insight, not innocence.

"When I knew another name," she said simply.

Chapter 12

"Rebeca, hurry now!" Gillian pulls her by the hand. Both stumble up the hill. So dark, so very dark.

"Comin' as fast as I can, lass."

Two girls running, running. Blizzard getting worse. Thorn grabs a long skirt. No time to stop. Red-headed Rebeca yanks on the skirt, tearing it. "Sorry!"

They stop to catch their breath. Smoke and flames rise over the trees. Screams, powerful shots come from the village. The girls look at each other, horrified. Guns? Were those guns they'd heard?

"Rebeca, what could it be?"

"I'm scared o' what we'll be findin'. Do we dare go on, Gillian?"

"No turnin' back now. We willna rest 'til we see what be happenin' to our folks."

More running. Dark-haired Gillian trips over a pile of stones. Up again. Running. Closer now. A cottage on fire. And another. Children screaming. Women running. One naked in the snow, bleeding, crying.

They stop. So cold. Why won't the snow quit?

"Rebeca?"

"Gillian?"
Panicked, they reach for each other. Two girls stand together,
shivering, too terrified to move any farther.

Maggie kept her eyes closed, although she'd been awake for
at least five or six minutes. Even her obsession with checking
the clock wasn't motivation enough to face the morning. Or the
remainder of the night, whichever the case may be. She'd gather
the courage to find out the time eventually.

Remnants of the dream lingered like the outline of a television
screen stared at too long. She tried to let the images go, but the
dark was now light and the light now dark. During the last four
years, this identical dream kept showing up over and over, each
time baffling Maggie to the point of madness. She could recite
every familiar scene, every word. When she wasn't dreaming it, she
spun it around and around in her mind, desperately prompting
the story to move forward.

But it remained stubbornly unyielding.

Maggie threw back the covers and sat on the edge of the
bed, waiting for her head to clear before finally opening her eyes.
Daylight overcame her. The faded half moon barely glistened just
to the east of the English walnut tree outside the bedroom. Ross
would be downstairs reading the sports page, thinking about all
he wanted to accomplish at the office that day. He might write
her a note telling her to have a good day. The smell of coffee,
predictably brewed too strong, reached her just then, nudging
her into movement. Eager to claim the warm spot left by her
mistress, Cleo gave one of her spontaneous feline yelps and leaped
up onto the bed. Maggie's feet searched the plush carpet for her
white terry cloth slippers, finding them under the nightstand
where she'd carefully placed them the previous evening.

Her feet were cold, as if she'd been standing in the snow.

Chapter 13

A few weeks after the curious incident at the parade, Maggie stopped by the Summerhill Public Library. Walking directly to the fiction shelves, she focused on acquiring a captivating story that might distract her from her dreams—the dreams which over the last five years had turned from intriguing to utterly frustrating, daily invading her every thought and action.

She searched intently for the latest mystery by Joy Fielding or John Dunning. *Nothing like solving a puzzle,* she thought. At twelve, she had sat in the elm tree in her front yard with her copy of *Clue of the Broken Locket,* pretending to be Nancy Drew on a sleuthing break, feeling worldly and sophisticated as she watched cars and neighbors go by from her lofty perch. Although the rigid limb was extremely uncomfortable, she stayed until her legs were numb, just to extend her fantasy. A decade or more later, she drove by that same childhood house, shocked to see her reading branch a mere five feet off the ground—not exactly the towering height she remembered. No wonder Darla Taylor, usually overprotective regarding her daughter's physical safety, had only smiled from the window while watching Maggie balance herself and scrape her legs going up and again coming back down.

It was actually Maggie's mother who had fostered her love of books. It wasn't uncommon for parents to read to their young children at bedtime, or chauffeur them to story time at the library. But Darla went further by encouraging Maggie to read anything she felt ready for as she got older, including controversial books that some parents thought should be banned. "No one is a better judge of books for you than you," she'd always say. It was one of her mother's gifts Maggie would forever cherish.

"Mrs. MacKenzie?"

Maggie knocked a book to the floor as she turned toward the sound of her name. Beside her was a strikingly handsome young man with short black curls. "Joey Martinez?"

Taller and darker than when he'd graduated from high school, Joey looked as if he'd stumbled upon a long-lost friend.

"Joey, you look wonderful. All grown up now, I guess. I can't believe we ran into each other."

He grinned, somewhat embarrassed. "Yeah, me neither."

"What are you doing now?"

"I'm in my third year at the University of Washington. I've been meaning to get in touch with you."

"Third year? How could that be? What program are you in?" Initially stunned Joey was in fact going to college, Maggie realized the look in his eyes was that of a young man who'd found his calling.

"Astronomy."

"Of course. I'm not surprised. What will you do with your degree?"

"Well, I haven't decided whether to go into research or teaching. Don't think I'd have the patience to teach high school kids, though. At least, not the ones like me." Another uncontrollable grin escaped, as Joey shifted from one foot to the other. "I'm thinking I'll need my master's degree to give myself some options. It's funny how much I love school now that I'm learning something so exciting."

"Well, Joey, I am absolutely thrilled. Just think." She took his elbow, guiding him toward a round table near the reference section.

They sat for a minute, neither one wanting to broach the inevitable topic. Maggie decided to dive right in. "Do you still have the same feelings you used to, Joey? I mean, about the moon and all?"

"Even stronger than before, I guess. But now there's something I didn't expect. The entire universe is just as fascinating to me as the moon—the planets, sun, other moons, other galaxies. The mystery and meaning of it all is like a giant riddle. I love trying to figure it out. I can barely think of anything else."

Maggie took a minute to consider what he'd said.

"What about you, Mrs. M.? How is your life going?" He was regarding her like a sharp attorney would a key witness, and she knew he'd refuse to let her sneak around an honest answer.

Still, she momentarily circumvented the subject. "You can call me Maggie now that I'm not your teacher, Joey."

"Oh, okay. If you want, uh, Maggie. So are you still at Summerhill High? And are you still having those dreams like before?"

One easy question, one not so easy. "Yes, I'll be there for a few more years. And the dreams … Well, I've had more since I saw you last, but not for a while." Not the whole truth, but close enough.

"Have you figured out what they mean? Are they still during the full moon?" Joey leaned forward.

Maggie shook her head in mild amusement. It occurred to her that Joey must have been wondering about this since they last saw each other. Her voice dropped lower as one of the older librarians, black-rimmed reading glasses balanced on the end of her pointed nose, walked by with a look that could quiet even a fussy toddler.

"So many questions," Maggie said. She took a deep breath. "At first the dreams were all during the full moon, but not lately. I thought I could accept them, but something feels different now, and I don't know what to think anymore. It's as if I've started over. And since I don't really understand what they might mean, or why I'm having them in the first place, for God's sake, it's a tad difficult discussing the subject."

"You've told Mr. MacKenzie about all this, right? How about Mrs. Kincaid? She's like your best friend, isn't she?"

"Sure she is." Maggie still thought of Claire that way, although their relationship had suffered an alteration after Julia came along. And, she supposed, the Bill Guthrie issue.

"Anything else you want to tell me?"

Hell, thought Maggie. *Why not?* She quickly summarized the story taking place in her dreams. She told Joey about Rebeca and Gillian, the closeness she felt to them, and the impending tragedy on that cold night. The tragedy she couldn't quite approach or begin to comprehend.

"Damn," he said. "I'm going to have to think about this."

Oh, Joey. This boy, this young man, had come into her life for a reason not totally clear to Maggie, but it really didn't matter. She couldn't be happier to see the direction his life was taking, or more grateful that it continued to coincide with hers, especially today. She suspected their paths would cross again and again, always with perfect timing. His fresh perspective and enthusiasm refreshed her, giving her life a nice jump-start whenever he showed up.

"Joey, will you let me know how you're doing? I'd love to hear more about your studies."

"Do you have a computer? We could e-mail."

"No, I'm dragging my feet on that one. How about regular letters with paper and pen for now?"

"No problem." Joey laughed. "And, Maggie? I think for now you should just relax. I've discovered that eventually things fall into place the way they're supposed to."

She dug around in her purse for a notepad. After exchanging addresses, she put her arm around his shoulders and squeezed tight. "You're probably right."

"I'll keep in touch," Joey said as he strode away.

"I'm counting on it."

Spencer and Cleo were lying side by side on the deck as Maggie peeked out the patio door. When she and Ross were home, the two acted like they had no interest whatsoever in each other, usually feigning disgust. But left alone, they showed their true colors. Spencer, now calm and mature, provided a gentle nature, as well as a furry pillow, for Cleo. He rose to greet Maggie, leaving the cat alarmed and suddenly in the mood for a bath.

Although Ross's truck was in the garage, he was nowhere in sight. It was only 5:15, but Maggie dug around the kitchen until she found something halfway decent for dinner—hot dogs, a can of shoe peg corn, and boxed macaroni and cheese. Ross suddenly stepped through the doorway covered in dirt, with Spencer, all his teeth showing in a magnificent dog grin, right next to him. Cleo sauntered behind.

Ross looked at his wife, at the empty stove, and then back at Maggie. "Is everything all right?" He glanced at the items gathered on the counter. "Is that what we're having for dinner?"

A few years ago they never would have considered eating a meal like this, but nowadays it seemed better than nothing. The expectations of chicken fettuccini, pork chops with hunter sauce and new potatoes, or stuffed Mexican shells with ground turkey had dwindled away over the months and years since Julia had been born, leaving such fancy dishes in a category for special company or Saturday night celebrations. Homemade casseroles and salad dressings remained teasers of a life that had somehow slipped away. The few changes Ross had hinted at on Julia's first birthday were now a dismal reality. Maggie was no longer interested in real cooking.

Ross sighed and muttered something about rose fertilizer before heading back outside.

"I'll have it ready in an hour," said Maggie, remembering a call she wanted to make. She picked up the phone and dialed Claire's number.

"Hi, there!" Claire answered. "It's great to hear from you. How are you anyway?"

"Pretty good, I suppose. I miss you, though. Can we have lunch sometime soon?" Maggie wanted to try Alexander's, the new bistro on Homestead Avenue.

"Oh, I'd love to, but it will have to wait a couple weeks. I'm leaving on Saturday," said Claire.

"Really? You and Jack taking a vacation?"

"Not exactly. I'll tell you everything another time, okay?"

Well, that was odd. Maggie wanted to inquire further, but Claire's tone insinuated the subject was closed for now. "All right. I hope we can catch up, though. Call me when you return?"

"Absolutely," Claire said. "And, Maggie, I really do want to talk to you."

"Great. See you soon then."

Maggie hung up and sat at the kitchen table, contemplating the conversation. *Was Claire going somewhere without Jack? By herself or with someone? And what was the big secret?* She poured iced tea into a tall glass decorated with bright watermelon slices and beach umbrellas, intending to relax a minute on the deck before boiling the macaroni water.

Spencer's bark caught her attention. His tail wagged incessantly as he and Ross appeared to be introducing themselves to their new neighbor. Ross turned to wave Maggie over, his eyes and smile as wide as a circus clown's.

"Maggie, Maggie!" he shouted to her. "This is Gina Lupinacci. She lives next door now."

Maggie guessed the attractive white-haired woman was in her late seventies. She extended her hand over the fence. "Pleased to meet you, Gina. You'll have to excuse my husband. I don't know why he's so stirred up."

"Gina invited us over for dinner tonight, honey," Ross said. "She's Italian, you know. And wow, doesn't something from her kitchen smell absolutely delicious? Isn't this great?"

Maggie glared at him. "But, Gina, we should be having you over to our house. Aren't you exhausted from moving?"

"Nah. Besides," Gina said, "my marinara sauce is simmering on the stove as we speak. It has a reputation, you know. If you two don't come over, I'll be eating spaghetti by myself for a week. The salad's in the fridge and the bread's all warm. You can bring a bottle of wine if it makes you feel better."

Ross nearly knocked Maggie over as he ran toward the house. "I'll go wash up," he hollered gleefully.

Chapter 14

As it turned out, Gina was right about the sauce—it was unbelievably delicious—and before the evening was over, Maggie felt her new neighbor would turn out to be right about many other things. She had resounding opinions on every topic and clearly felt entitled to express them. Her pleasantly round build, emerald eyes, and full head of thick white hair commanded complete attention. The lady was refreshingly feisty and spirited without being offensive. Her small house was filled with mementos she'd collected from around the world, in travels both with and without her husband, who had passed away fifteen years earlier. Above the fireplace, Gina displayed scads of family photos in old wooden frames, the eyes of the Italian ancestors holding secrets evident only to the few remaining descendants who had known them. Maggie knew this fascinating woman must be filled with stories waiting for a receptive ear.

"Tell me about your family," she prompted. Ross, belly satisfied, had excused himself right after dinner, leaving the two women alone to visit while he went home to his roses.

Gina jumped up, waving her hands at various old portraits as she enthusiastically related tale after tale of scandalous affairs and the shady financial dealings of one relative after another. "But, honey, even through the tough times, there was always an endless supply of good food and real love. A family's gotta have that no matter what."

"Did you have a happy childhood?" asked Maggie, thoroughly enjoying her entertaining new friend. She settled in on the sofa. "What were your parents like?"

"Oh, they were wonderful. Very loving, hard-working people. Came to this country when I was about five." She snickered. "When I was older, they confessed to me that I was conceived in a vat of grapes in Solerno. Can you picture that?"

Maggie laughed so hard, her face hurt.

"Imagine the mess," Gina went on matter-of-factly. "Maybe it explains my passionate spirit. At my age, I prefer to keep busy with decent charity work or a rowdy political brawl. Whether you're young or old, every single day is an opportunity to make a difference for someone. Don't you agree?" She plopped down next to Maggie and threw her arms around her in a big hug.

Tears dribbled down Maggie's cheeks. She was stunned that in a matter of hours, she already felt a deep, genuine affection for this woman. It was as if Gina was meant to fill a hole in her heart—a hole she hadn't really known was there until this moment. Gina produced a hanky with the initials GL, and Maggie wiped her eyes. "Sorry. I don't know what's the matter with me."

"No problem," replied Gina. She leaned back to get a better look at Maggie's expression, gently squeezing both her shoulders. "Hmm ... is there something you want to share with me about your own family now?"

Maggie sniffled and cleared her throat. "Well, there's Julia."

"And who might she be?"

"My very special granddaughter. You'll have to meet her," Maggie began. And she proceeded to tell Gina about the previous Christmas, when Julia insisted the family cut way back on the commercialism of the holiday. She suggested only handmade, heartfelt gifts, with leftover money going to less fortunate families. Or as she put it, "giving more like Jesus would give."

"Sounds like quite a girl. Did she want to give up the tree too?"

"She finally caved in on that one, much to her mother's relief."

Gina nodded. "Good decision. So you just have the one daughter?"

"Yes. She's actually my stepdaughter, but Ross and I raised her together." Maggie wished Kellie and Julia could be there right now in Gina's living room. They would love her. "I'm pretty lucky."

"And what about your parents? Do they live close by?" Gina fired off the questions, apparently hungry to learn all she could.

Maggie examined the cover of *Italian Cooking & Living* on the coffee table, half-expecting to find a word or two to get her started. But, of course, there were none.

"They're gone, aren't they?" Gina said.

"Died in a car accident when I was twenty-three."

Gina frowned. "I'll bet they were wonderful."

"Both of them were, yes."

"And you really miss your father, but it's the loss of your mother that's been the biggest heartbreak."

Maggie couldn't believe Gina would say that. "How did you know?"

"A girl needs her mother no matter how old she is." Gina scooted closer, pulling Maggie toward her. "Being an orphan is one of the worst experiences in life, isn't it?"

"I hate it!" sobbed Maggie. She let herself be cradled and rocked against Gina's gigantic breasts until her eyes were dry.

They cried and talked and laughed and talked some more, until Maggie realized Ross must be wondering why she had not come home.

"Ross is nice," said Gina, walking her to the back door. "But when was the last time he ate? That man can put away the food, I'll tell you."

Lighter and freer than she had felt in years, Maggie strolled across the yard, a crescent moon hanging above her like a lopsided smile.

Chapter 15

Maggie decided to take Joey's advice and lighten up. The evening with Gina had released a substantial amount of pent-up emotion, and she felt better than she had in years. She found it as effortless to slip back into her pre-Julia lifestyle as one returning to a former neighborhood. Cutting her hair and nails short again, digging out her traditional "teacher" clothes, as well as setting up the ironing board, felt deliciously satisfying.

Maggie swore she heard Ross's audible sigh of relief as his favorite recipes began reappearing on the supper table. Obviously hoping to sustain this surprising development, he would merely smile and say, "Terrific meal, honey. You've always been an exceptional cook."

He broached the subject of their retirement, still awhile off but exciting to consider all the same. Surprisingly, he announced he might be ready to give up the demands of his garden in a year or two and look for a condo. Maggie picked up European travel brochures. They imagined Kellie remarrying some wonderful newspaper editor or investment banker. And Julia would be a teenager in a few years—imagine that! Why, there was no end to the possibilities of a gratifying future for their little family, they thought.

Relieved to be back in a routine that actually made sense, Maggie returned to the familiar world of Summerhill High School at the end of the summer. She welcomed it as her refuge, thriving in hallways filled with loud, boisterous teenagers who longed simply to find a place, any place, to fit in. She witnessed this process every day, from the flirting eyes and conspicuous physical contact between potential love interests, to the brilliant students like Beth Shaw, a straight-laced, clear-skinned girl. Purposely missing questions in Claire's English class, she longed to appear average enough to be accepted by the three back row girls who barely earned Cs. Maggie knew the games they played, but those games comforted her. They were what she expected.

Even the same frustrating dream, playing over and over again, slid into the category of predictable life.

In spite of their good intentions, Maggie and Claire did not find the time to get together until November. They met for lunch one chilly Saturday at Alexander's, the spot Maggie had had in mind before Claire went on her mysterious summer trip. Claire nearly glowed as she scooted into her side of the booth.

"Wow," Maggie said, amazed. "You look so … healthy."

Claire took the menu from the waitress and glanced at the salad choices before answering, "As a matter of fact, I have lost a few pounds. Thanks for noticing. Somehow my attitude about food has changed. You know how they say it's not what you're eating, but what's eating you?"

A year earlier, Maggie knew Claire would have gone right to the burger and fries section of the menu. Now she could hardly wait to discover what exactly had been "eating" her friend. They gave the waitress, Della, as her nametag prominently displayed, their identical orders of chicken Caesar salad, dressing on the side, decaf coffee, and handed back their menus.

Claire began. "Maggie, I feel almost ashamed we've been so out of touch. I hope you know it's nothing you've said or done.

It's just you've been extra busy since Julia came along, plus I've had some things of my own to deal with."

Thankful for the opening, Maggie said, "I feel the same. Do you want to talk about those things?"

Laughing, Claire tore off the paper band around her napkin-encased silverware. "Nothing like getting right to the point!"

"Well, we used to be able to tell each other anything. I don't see any reason for that to change just because we haven't seen each other in a while, do you?"

"No, of course not," Claire said. "Are you ready for this?"

"Oh, believe me, Claire, nothing could shock me anymore." Maggie shook her head.

"Well, you know when I went away last summer? I was in New Orleans to see Bill Guthrie."

"Get out!" Maggie slapped the table hard enough to rattle the knives and forks.

"Remember the time I told you there was someone I felt close to and I couldn't explain why? Like you and Julia? It was him. It was Bill." Claire's shoulders visibly relaxed. She stirred some artificial sweetener into the coffee the waitress brought to the table and took a sip.

"I suspected this, you know," Maggie told her.

"I figured that's why you encouraged me to call him. How did you know?"

Maggie looked around the restaurant and saw only a thirtyish man and woman at a table near the front door, but still leaned closer to Claire. "When I called him about the science materials, he confessed to me."

"Confessed? Confessed what?"

"That he had the same weird feeling about you."

Claire sighed. "Well, naturally I'm aware of that now. But why didn't you tell me back then?"

"I don't know. I just wasn't quite sure how to handle the information, except to persuade you to get in touch with him.

I suppose I was confused about everything going on in my own life too."

Claire went on to say that she had barely stopped thinking about Bill the last couple of years, to the point of not thinking much at all about her own husband, Jack. Eventually, she couldn't stand it any longer, so she arranged to go to New Orleans without Jack's knowledge. She and Bill spent a week together, in a strictly platonic manner, she was quick to explain. The two of them hashed everything out, and at the end of the week, Claire was entirely ready to come back to Summerhill and Jack.

"Wait, wait," Maggie interrupted. "Where did Jack think you were?"

Della placed their salads in front of them, waiting for the conversation to continue. Maggie and Claire turned to face her, smiling. Like a child discovering a closed sign in the candy store window, Della walked back to the kitchen, scowling.

Claire leaned across the table. "He thought I went to a spa to get all rejuvenated and pampered." She giggled. "Well, the trip *was* a type of therapy."

Maggie grinned. "Very clever."

"I thought so. Besides, I didn't want Jack to think I was having an affair or something wild like that. He blames every goofy thing I do these days on menopause anyway."

They laughed. That was a topic for another lunch date.

Maggie drizzled a spoonful of dressing on her salad while pressing for more details. "But you haven't told me what you and Bill talked about. Did you come up with any answers to this familiarity you've always felt with each other? Did you figure out what it all means?"

There was Della again, persistent as ever. "Can I get you ladies anything else?" she asked, ripping off two pages from her order pad.

"No thanks," Maggie and Claire said in unison. Again they waited until she slunk away.

"What we figured out," Claire said, lowering her voice, "was that we couldn't really explain it and it really didn't matter."

"Well, I'll be." It sounded so tempting to Maggie. Let it go. It doesn't matter.

"We never would've been satisfied, though, if we hadn't spent the time together and talked about it openly like we did. It would've nagged at us forever. The more we admitted our feelings toward each other, the more we discovered we were like brother and sister, not star-crossed lovers. We enjoyed simply talking about everyday things, watching movies, eating, laughing. We don't understand where the feelings of knowing each other so well came from, but we agreed it wasn't worth worrying about. The feelings are there. Period."

Maggie's eyes widened.

"Perhaps later on in our lives," Claire went on, "we'll discover some rational explanation for it, but right now we can accept it for what it is—something unique, mysterious, and positive. The world is full of mystifying events, Maggie. I don't think we're meant to comprehend every one of them." Claire retrieved her lip gloss from the bottom of her purse. "There's one other thing."

Uh-oh, thought Maggie. "What is it?"

"Bill's ex-wife. He feels terrible about leaving her now. He was so confused a few years ago, he thought he was doing the right thing. Apparently she's having a pretty rough time of it. He's going to ask if she'll take him back."

"Holy shit. And Jack?" Maggie asked. "Do you still feel the same about him?"

"You know, if I had met Bill before I met Jack, I could have easily married him. It would've been like marrying a best friend. But that's not what happened. I never stopped loving Jack, and I seem to appreciate him even more after this. He is so funny and smart and kind and, well, sexy. I just can't get enough of him lately." Claire let out a delicate snort.

Maggie choked on her sip of coffee. What a hoot. She realized how much she'd missed these tell-all conversations with Claire.

How could she have let her friend go through this all alone? "I'm so sorry I wasn't there for you, Claire."

"No big deal. I knew you would be if I just said the word." Claire dabbed at the corners of her mouth with her napkin. "Now then, how about you and Julia? How is that going?"

"Well … I've been having some pretty unsettling dreams which may or may not have something to do with Julia, but I like the conclusion you and Bill came up with. I can't explain any of it either, but you've convinced me it really doesn't matter. I'm going to forget all about it," Maggie declared.

"But this is totally different! Have you discussed it at all with Ross or Kellie? Have you truly worked through this? Aren't you curious?" Claire stopped talking as Maggie began fiddling in her purse for a piece of gum.

"It's fine, honestly." Maggie's tone made it clear the conversation was at an end.

They left Della a nice tip, mostly in appreciation for finally leaving them alone.

In the parking lot, Claire stopped at Maggie's car. "I've applied for a different job starting next semester."

"You mean a different subject than English?"

"That's part of it. I want to be a remedial reading teacher. There's an opening at the middle school that begins next semester."

"What brought this on? How can you think of working with those nutty middle school kids? When will we ever see each other?" To Maggie, this astonishing announcement practically topped the one about Bill Guthrie.

Claire hugged her, saying, "Oh, you know the amount of whining I've done over the years about the workload of an English teacher. All those essays to wade through and literature to analyze. I'm getting too old to keep up with it. Maybe I can make a difference by helping some twelve-year-old become a better reader."

"Lord. I suppose I should've seen this coming," Maggie muttered.

"Just part of my new perspective on life," said Claire. "I don't want to turn into one of those old, cranky, burned-out teachers who *need* to retire long before they *want* to. By the way, I thought I might start coming to your church once in a while. We can see each other there."

Maggie jerked her head around. "Really?"

"Really. Jack said he might come along as well. But, Maggie?"

"Yes?"

"I want you to reconsider the way you're handling this issue with Julia. I don't believe you should let go of it until you've answered some questions for yourself. There might be some unresolved issues you need to deal with before you can completely leave it alone. I learned with Bill that you shouldn't ignore your gut feelings. Ever." Claire beeped her car remote and opened the driver's door. "I'll be praying for you."

Praying? Claire?

Stunned, Maggie watched her drive away. She turned toward her Subaru but then returned the keys to her coat pocket and paced back and forth next to the car. Questions tumbled around in her head like sneakers in a clothes dryer. Just when she thought she was finally accepting the situation, Claire's admonishment had her wondering again. Where did the dreams come from? Who were those two girls? Why had Julia acted so strange when she saw the bagpipers? Why did Claire have to come along and dig up all these bewildering emotions when she wanted them tucked safely away?

As if responding to Maggie's internal tug of war, a 1979 Chevy Impala roared into the empty parking slot she was occupying, forcing her to jump back against her car. A boy with spiky bleached blond hair slammed on his brakes roughly two feet from her knees and rolled the window down. Over the inevitable heart-pounding bass of hip-hop music, he yelled, "Hey, lady! Are you comin' or goin'?"

Chapter 16

"Gillian, be ye warm enough?"

"Ay, Rebeca, as warm as I might expect, considerin'."

The girls huddle together inside a gray stone church. Pull wool coats tight. More children, some with mothers, others alone, all shivering, hungry. All scared, sad.

"Gilli, do ye think it be true? Folks in the village really be dead?"

"I think we have to believe it, Rebeca. The worst part is your own da missin' and possibly me entire family gone. But why? 'Tis breakin' me heart."

"But 'tis three days now. Canna we go back to see for ourselves? Maybe 'tis not true after all. And what about me mam back home? How will she take the news? How will she care for the wee ones by herself now? How will she find me, Gilli?"

"Me neighbor, Mrs. Saunders, she told us all she seen—me da and me brother Brody lyin' dead next to her own husband. And later she found me mam and me other brother, Kendric, in the snow. They must've run from the house with naught but their nightclothes on. Mrs. Saunders wouldna lie about such a horrible thing, Rebeca."

"You're right, Gillian. I must face it. Me da is surely dead."

"So sorry, I am. 'Tis lucky we have each other. Barely made it to this church in the blizzard. We must be strong now, we must."

Tears come. Won't stop. Terrible aching in the chest.

"I'm hungry," both girls say together. Small giggle stifles the crying.

Icy wind, snow swirling into the room. Woman bolts door behind her, drops three rabbits on the floor. "Supper, anyone?" Mrs. Saunders asks.

Twelve girls shouting, running, bringing wood.

Stove pops, crackles. Delicious smell.

"Mrs. Saunders, might we be helpin' ye?" Rebeca asks.

"Sweet girls, to be certain. Even with the misfortune barely behind us."

Gillian steps forward. "Can ye tell us more o' what ye know? Who did the killin'? Why did they do it?"

The woman sits. Pulls both girls toward her. "Now, now," she says. "There'll be a time for ye to learn more. Today we need to be thinkin' what to do next. Mrs. Henderson tells me bright young lasses like yourselves could be workin' in the city mindin' the bairns o' rich folk."

The city? So far away? Rebeca and Gillian look into each other's eyes. How would they get there with no money or food? What would become of them?

Maggie felt a soft kiss brush her cheek. She sat up in bed, instantly wishing for a camera. Clouds were nonexistent in the blue black sky on this Friday night, and one of the biggest, brightest moons she'd ever seen appeared to be within arm's reach. Venus loomed just to the north, a twinkling, flashing beacon pleading to be recognized for its own magnificent splendor.

In spite of the dream's disturbing overtones, Maggie felt a total sense of relief in finally having it. The brilliant full moon had at last brought her beyond the spinning wheels of the dream with no end. She had no choice at this point except to move forward. These girls, for whatever reason, were deeply and irrefutably inside her heart. She cared too much about Rebeca and Gillian to desert them now.

Chapter 17

As time went on, Julia's intuitive nature and perception of the world became more and more apparent. She drew people to her in such a way that settled nerves, renewed spirits, and left everyone craving her companionship. But as she got older, it was still her grandmother's company she preferred.

"Gammy, do you love me?" she asked one afternoon at the lake. She and Maggie had finished their picnic and were throwing popcorn to the ducks.

"Honey, you know I do. I tell you all the time," Maggie said. "Why would you ask such a thing?"

"Well, I love Mommy and Daddy and Grandpa and Spencer and Cleo, but I love you different. I think I've loved you longer."

Longer? What an extraordinary thing to say. Maggie continued to be amazed at this surprisingly perceptive girl in denim jeans and a yellow T-shirt. In one sentence, Julia had simplified everything Maggie agonized over.

"Julia, darling," Maggie started, "I understand what you mean and I feel the same way about you. I'm not sure why, but I do."

"It doesn't mean we don't love the others just as much," Julia replied. She ate one kernel of popcorn and threw another for a duck.

"That's absolutely correct," said Maggie, hoping Julia would voice additional insight.

"We shouldn't worry about it. Maybe a dream will explain it."

What did she say? Maggie was too startled to question her further. She watched as Julia tossed the remaining popcorn out into the water.

Julia's ability to cut through the peripheral details of life and focus on the essentials astounded her family, but it didn't compare to her talent in playing the flute. At the beginning of second grade, the school music teacher brought in twelve instruments for the younger students to try out, hoping to spark some early interest for the band. But Mr. Crenshaw didn't anticipate the feisty red-headed girl who walked right past him, picked up the flute, looked it over, put her lips and fingers in the correct position, and played like she'd been taking private lessons all her life. The rest of the class stared. Mr. Crenshaw temporarily froze and then scuttled, a noticeable hop to his step, to the telephone. Not one to miss a beat under the most unusual of circumstances, Julia's classroom teacher, Miss Hamilton, whipped out her list of parent phone numbers and handed it to the dumbfounded music instructor.

Twenty minutes later, when Kellie hung up the phone, her jaw still down around her knees, she dialed her mother's direct line to the high school library.

"Guess what she's done now?" she asked Maggie. And they laughed over what must have been looks of pure astonishment on the teachers' faces.

Never lacking for a cause, the next fall Julia organized a class protest against door-to-door school fund-raisers. According to her teacher, she'd announced that adults should figure out how to get money for schools, not kids. She and her following of friends sneaked inside the school during recess one day and painted six hot pink poster board signs, stating No More Cookie Dough Sales, before Mrs. Shaw discovered them. Kellie agreed with the teacher that Julia's passion would serve her well in later years, but right now the chance of overruling the school board on the fund-raising policy would be like asking a newly licensed teenager to give up the car keys. It just wasn't going to happen.

Meanwhile, Maggie traveled up and down the exasperating path set before her. The dream girls continued to fascinate her, showing up with an occasional full moon, but the time between dreams grew longer and longer. Plus, the story bounced around, repeating dreams she'd already had, and only occasionally adding a few minor details. She still longed for a sensible explanation as to why she was having them at all. A clear reason. A meaning. Was it too much to ask after so many years?

Having just renewed her friendship with Claire and then immediately losing her to another school disappointed Maggie. But Claire kept her promise about showing up at church once in a while, prompting Maggie to continue taking advantage of the peace of mind she found in the confines of the high-beamed ceiling, stained glass, and celestial music. The women weren't always able to convince Ross and Jack of the benefits of regular attendance, but Kellie and Julia joined them on an occasional Sunday.

On this gorgeous morning in mid-February, nine-year-old Julia stopped in front of Reverend Chamberlain on the way out the door. Looking straight up into his face, she declared, "Reverend, you have a very nice church here, but I don't think Jesus would've liked so much attention. Wouldn't it be better if we were all out doing nice things for other people instead?"

Kellie turned to Maggie and Claire and rolled her eyes.

Claire, always and forever an English teacher, whispered to Maggie, "She is so articulate for her age."

Reverend Chamberlain squatted down closer to Julia, placing one hand on her shoulder. "Julia, dear, it would surely be a wonderful way to spend a Sunday morning. However, lots of people feel a need to come together to reinforce—by that I mean, to strengthen—their faith in God. It helps them get through the tough things in life. I know you will figure out what is best for *you* to do."

A perfect answer, thought Maggie.

Julia patted his hand and smiled. "Thank you for understanding. And, Reverend?"

"Yes."

"I know what the word 'reinforce' means." And off she went to wait in the car, leaving the others doubled over laughing.

Reverend Chamberlain, undeniably amused, turned to Maggie. "Would you have time to stop by my office next week? There's something I want to talk to you about."

Too baffled to speak, Maggie only nodded in agreement.

While Ross washed dishes that night, Maggie retreated to the den and turned on her computer. After much prodding from Kellie, who had argued Julia would benefit from a computer to use for her school work, Ross and Maggie had finally relented to join the technological age. The headache in the electronics store was nothing compared to the one they suffered while assembling the thing, but now they both depended on it more than they had ever imagined. Maggie believed e-mail was the greatest invention since the telephone.

She checked her in-box and found a message from Joey Martinez.

Hey, Maggie,
Hope you're doing okay. How's the family?

Well, a master's degree is finally within reach. Hooray! It took awhile, but has definitely been worth it. I have an interview next month with NASA—can you believe it? I'm hoping to start at the ground level there and work on my PhD in the evenings.

Yes, there's a girlfriend in the picture. More on her later, ha, ha.

Say, I'm driving up your way a week from Monday to visit my parents. Will you be around? There's something I want to tell you.

Joey

P.S. Remind me to talk to you about the plane of the ecliptic.

Plane of the what? Was he taking a trip somewhere?

Maggie leaned back in the desk chair. So both Reverend Chamberlain and Joey wanted to talk to her about something. How interesting. The same thing? Two different things? To her knowledge, they didn't even know each other. She left the computer on for the night and turned out the den light. But not before checking the calendar for the current lunar phase.

Chapter 18

"Rebeca? Rebeca! Wake up! We be gettin' close!"

"What?" The red-haired girl raises her head from the rail of the wagon. Bump, bump, bump over the rough, icy road. Hills covered in patches of snow, dead trees, and crinkled-up heather. She rubs her eyes. Looks over at her friend. "Canna tell if you're laughin' or cryin' about it, Gillian."

"Excited is all. Glad to be gettin' a fresh start and leavin' the sorrow behind us." Her brunette hair blows in all directions. Pulls the blanket tighter around her shoulders.

Bitter snow swirls around the six girls in the wagon. Mrs. Saunders looks back at them, smiles with bluish lips. Snaps the reins at the two old horses carrying them farther and farther away from the small village.

"Ye be peaceful it seems, Gillian. How can ye just forget about what we saw back there? Your entire family is gone!"

"Rebeca, I'll never be forgettin' it. I just want to have a good life in spite o' it."

They ride in silence. Other girls try to huddle closer. One or two cry. Deep cold and sadness surround them.

"Gillian?"

"Yes."

"What do ye think about me mam? When she hears what happened, she'll be bloomin' gyte, she will. I know she'll be wonderin' about me. How can I get to her now? 'Tis breaking me heart to think o' her worryin'. I can see her, I can, puttin' on a kettle for tea, pacin' back and forth, back and forth, back and forth. She'll wear a hole in the floor, she will."

Gillian pulls her friend closer. Puts one arm around her under the blanket. "I know how ye must feel. We have no choice, Rebeca. We must go with Mrs. Saunders to Inverness. She says 'tis not safe for us to return home right now."

"But why wouldna it be safe?"

Gillian shakes her head. "Mrs. Saunders be explainin' eventually. After we settle and earn some spendin' money, then I'll help ye figure out how to get word to your mam. At the orphanage school we can play music, didna ye hear? I can learn the flute, just like I always dreamed. Love the sound as much as the bagpipes, I do. For now, we must stick together to make the best o' things."

Rebeca wipes her eye with the back of her cold hand. "We will, Gilli."

Wagon jerks. Stops. Mrs. Saunders gets out and looks at the back left wheel. "Just needs a bit o' tightenin'," she says. "No worries, lasses. We'll be there soon enough."

Rolling down a hill. Wheel steady now. Snow stops. Clouds blow away. Sunshine feels heavenly on the face. Sparkling river. Cottages.

"Be it Inverness, Gillian?"

"'Tis, indeed. What a braw glen to start our new life, eh Rebeca?"

The red-haired girl pulls the blanket up to her chin. Tries to smile.

Maggie breathed a sigh of relief as she dangled her legs over the side of the bed. Temporarily, at least, the long dry spell between new dreams was finally over. Ross grunted and twitched his feet under the covers.

Wide awake now, with no chance of going back to sleep anytime soon, Maggie grabbed her robe and made her way down the hall to check on Julia in the guest room. Kellie had gone off to Seattle on a promising date with a lawyer, leaving Julia with her parents. Julia had begged for an evening of Hawaiian pizza and *E.T.* A clever debater, she got her way, of course, but only after pledging to help Ross figure out how to work their DVD player. It was 11:15 before Julia was tucked in. Maggie doubted she had moved a single muscle all night.

As she gently pushed open the guest room door, Maggie was shocked to discover Julia standing by the window, her face toward the spectacular night sky.

"Honey, are you all right?"

At first Julia stood silently before the golden moon, which on this night resembled a foil-wrapped chocolate coin, with dents and creases hinting at secrets inside. Maggie easily maneuvered across the illuminated floor, stepping over Julia's shoes, flute, and overnight bag. She tried again. "Sweetheart, couldn't you sleep?"

Turning toward her grandmother, her tousled scarlet hair haloed about her face, Julia asked, "Gammy, where exactly is Inverness?"

Chapter 19

Because the next morning was Sunday, a day when Maggie would usually see Claire at church, Maggie decided to include her friend in the family meeting. Besides, Maggie knew she wouldn't be in the mood to repeat everything later. Better to get it all out at once, and do it right the first time. And, of course, Claire would welcome the chance to be involved in any potential drama.

Kellie, another key component of the gathering, pulled into the driveway less than fifteen minutes after hanging up her phone, although Maggie had assured her several times that Julia was absolutely fine.

Patiently awaiting the particular reason for the conference, Ross kept busy by complying with Maggie's request that he put on a pot of coffee, as well as popping two tubes of Pillsbury Orange Rolls into the oven. Maggie hoped everyone's anxiety levels would drop when they were confronted with the irresistible, comforting aromas. Furthermore, she was confident this would be a simple issue with a simple solution. She wouldn't be concerned about it at all if it wasn't for Julia.

Spencer and Cleo, keenly aware of the charge in the atmosphere, lay side by side on the green and white oval rug in front of the fireplace, waiting to see what might transpire. The others took various seats around the living room.

In the shower earlier, Maggie had rehearsed a tidy speech in her head, but Julia beat her to the first punch. "I convinced Gammy to have a meeting this morning, because she and I discovered last night we've been having the same dreams."

Kellie stared wide-eyed at her daughter, and then at Maggie, and then at Ross.

Looking down at her feet, Claire stifled a smirk.

"What kind of dreams, sweetie?" asked Ross.

"The dreams with the two girls I told you about before," Maggie answered for her. "It's really no big deal."

"If it's no big deal, then why did you call us all together?" asked Claire.

Momentarily, Maggie regretted inviting Claire. She hoped she wouldn't blow this all out of proportion. Keeping her attention on her granddaughter, she replied, "Julia urged me to. She thinks the dreams mean something important."

"Why don't we allow Julia to answer for herself, Mom?" Kellie asked. "What do you want to tell us about these dreams, baby?"

Julia rose and immediately walked over to the front of the fireplace. If there had been a podium handy, she would've casually taken the microphone. Maggie, suddenly nervous about what her granddaughter might divulge, also stood up. Claire and Kellie each took a hand, gently pulling her back down to the sofa. Sensing the rising level of tension, Spencer and Cleo moved over to Ross's leather chair, forming furry bookends around his shoes.

Julia resumed. "It's like they're short snippets of a story—chapters of a book, so to speak. The dreams involve two girls, around twelve or thirteen I believe, who become good friends. They lived a long time ago, somewhere in Scotland where they say 'loch' for 'lake.' Anyway, the dreams tell about some kind of murders in the village where one of them lives. Lots of people were killed. We don't know why yet."

"They're just dreams," Maggie muttered, folding her arms in front of her chest.

Ross glared at her. "But you told me before that the dreams scare you and make you feel strange the next day. Don't you want to get to the bottom of this, Maggie?"

"Yes. No. Oh, hell, I don't know."

"We have to, Gammy," said Julia. "You know we do."

Everyone, except Maggie, leaned forward to focus on Julia. They realized any word of encouragement was unnecessary, since there would be no stopping her now.

Julia faced her audience. "You've gotta admit it's pretty weird to find out Gammy and I are dreaming the exact same dreams. I don't think that usually happens to people, do you?"

Maggie sat with her mouth tightly pursed, but everyone else looked at each other in agreement. How true, how true, their expressions seemed to confirm.

"There's more," Julia continued. "Isn't it just a bit bizarre that the dreams are a continuing story of someone's life? Have any of *you* dreamed like that? Have you?"

"Certainly not," said Kellie.

"Definitely strange," Ross confirmed.

They all looked at Claire. "No, not very common," she said. "But apparently it is happening."

"So it seems," Julia replied. "And there's something else."

All right, Maggie thought. *This was enough.* She couldn't stay put any longer. Leaping up before Claire and Kellie could grab her, and sending the startled cat and dog scrambling out of the living room, Maggie marched up to face Julia head on, her back to her husband, daughter, and best friend. She stood there, jaw set tight, knees shaking, already denying the words Julia was about to say next.

Julia took a deep breath and reached for her grandmother's hands. They held each other's gazes as nine-year-old Julia, her tone and demeanor clearly confirming a maturity and wisdom far beyond her years, announced, "They're like us, Gammy. Those two girls are like us."

A gasp escaped Kellie.

Julia tried to continue. "One girl has red hair and the other has dark brown, and I think—"

"No, no, that's not right," Maggie interrupted. "How could that be?" She jerked her hands away from Julia's and covered her face. Her entire body trembling, she latched onto a bookcase to steady herself.

Without a word, Kellie and Claire hopped up, clearing the way for Ross, who quickly grasped Maggie's arm and steered her back to the sofa. He placed a pillow behind her back, supplied her with a cup of cooling coffee and an orange roll from the tray on the side table, and kissed her cheek. Then he stepped back to have a good look at her.

"There, now," he said. "You'll feel better in a minute so we can discuss this."

Maggie astonished herself by taking a swig of coffee, followed by bolting down not one, but two orange rolls. She'd forgotten how delicious they were. Someone handed her a box of tissues. Ross was right; she was starting to feel much better already. "Sorry about that," she managed to say.

The four people Maggie loved most in the world looked at her, their expressions revealing a calm serenity that struck her as rather unnatural, considering the topic at hand. The inconceivable gradually occurred to her. "Surely you don't believe Julia and I are really the girls in the dreams. Do you?"

Claire seized the opportunity. "Maggie, I know it seems crazy, but I do believe something like that is possible. I don't know how or why, but, yes, I think it could be true."

Maggie turned toward Ross and Kellie. "What about you two?"

"Go ahead, Dad," said Kellie, waving one hand in the air. "You tell her."

Ross sat on the sofa next to Maggie. "Mag, I know I should've mentioned this before, but, well, sometimes you talk in your sleep. You know, when you're having these dreams."

"And?" she demanded.

"And, well, I've heard you say the girls' names."

"You mean Rebeca and Gillian? So?"

Ross looked at Kellie, who raised one eyebrow as a go-ahead sign.

"Sometimes you mutter Rebeca. And sometimes ..." He paused, a perplexing tone of fear and disbelief creeping into his voice.

Maggie tried to finish for him. "And sometimes Gillian?"

"Well, yes, but ..." He looked all around the room, as if to make sure no one else had slipped in unnoticed. Lowering his voice anyway, he finally said, "Sometimes it's Julia."

Flabbergasted, Maggie could barely speak. "What did you say?"

"And I've heard Julia call out Gammy," Kellie said. "Dad and I have already discussed this, Mom. We just didn't know what to do about it."

Silence seeped like floodwaters into every corner of the room. Julia continued to stand in front of the fireplace by herself. Maggie felt her penetrating stare but couldn't bring herself to return it. Finally Ross got up, handed Claire the tray of orange rolls to pass around, and went into the kitchen to make a fresh pot of coffee. Julia followed him.

"Mom," Kellie said, "think about the other things that have happened—Julia's reaction to the bagpipers at the parade, the extreme closeness you've felt with each other since the night she was born, the realness of the dreams, the fact you're both having them. And I'll bet anything there's probably stuff you've neglected to mention. It's definitely not your everyday deal." Kellie picked up an orange roll. "Maybe we can't explain it just yet, but obviously it has some kind of significance for the two of you. I don't think it's healthy to just push it away and pretend it doesn't exist."

"Kellie's absolutely right," Claire added. "I know from personal experience that trying to ignore these kinds of situations only adds to the frustration and confusion of it all."

The two women waited while Maggie sat quietly, scarcely breathing.

At last she said, "I've tried to handle this every way possible— one day totally denying there's anything unusual going on, and the next day embracing the situation to the point of obsession. But today it's become so overwhelming, I can't think straight. So for now, I don't wish to discuss it further." And with that, she left the room.

When Ross and Julia returned from the kitchen, they found Kellie and Claire still staring after her.

Chapter 20

Reverend Chamberlain, his arms wrapped around an enormous stack of file folders and papers, pushed his office door open with his left elbow. Red-faced and panting from the trek to the church basement and back, he appeared startled to find a woman examining the rows of books on his far wall. Although he couldn't see her face, he evidently knew who she was. "Welcome, Maggie. If you're checking to see if they're in any type of logical order, I'm afraid you're going to be disappointed."

Maggie looked over her shoulder. "Hello, Reverend. And no, the order of your library is really the least of my concerns this morning."

The reverend set his load of reference materials in the corner chair, where they would remain until later in the day when he wrote next Sunday's sermon. Brushing back the long strands of hair over a balding spot, he motioned for Maggie to sit down. "I thought I might see you today."

Maggie sat. "Oh really? Did Claire give you a call by any chance?"

"How did you know?" Smiling, the reverend eased into the swivel chair behind his desk.

"I suspected you might be the lucky one to hear all about what happened in our living room yesterday." Maggie started to pick at a hangnail but quickly clutched both hands together in her lap instead.

Reverend Chamberlain took a blue pen out of a cup and began doodling on his desk pad. "So I was."

Each waited for the other to speak.

"Do any of those books on your shelves have some answers for me?" asked Maggie at last.

"Possibly. I think we need to start by—" Reverend Chamberlain's sentence was suspended by a friendly male voice coming from the doorway.

"Hello, Maggie. I stopped at school, but you'd already left. I thought I saw your car out front. Same one you had ten years ago, isn't it?" The tall, dark-complexioned man walked into the room, bending down to hug Maggie before offering his hand to Reverend Chamberlain. "Hi, I'm Joey Martinez. Sorry to barge in like this. I have a bad habit of showing up unexpectedly."

"So we finally meet, Joey. Maggie's bragged to me about your recent accomplishments. And don't worry about popping in like this. I think your timing is perfect."

Dumbfounded and slightly suspicious, Maggie asked, "Did you two plan this?"

"No," Joey assured her. "Should we have?"

"A week ago I would have known how to respond to such a question. I thought my life was under control. I was coming to terms with the dreams, even looking forward to them, really. And it was so much easier to merely enjoy my unique relationship with Julia, rather than constantly wonder about it. But now? Now I feel like someone tossed all the pieces of this puzzle into a food processor without any regard to the outcome. Am I just supposed to sit around and wait to see what happens next?" Fighting back her emotions, Maggie sniffled and sighed.

Joey plunked down next to her, noticeably perplexed. "I know you've been having unusual dreams over the years, but it sounds like I've missed some critical details."

"You go ahead and tell him, Reverend," Maggie prompted.

"Of course. You're aware that for several years Maggie has been dreaming about two young girls in Scotland. Now she's learned that her granddaughter, Julia, has been having the identical dreams. That, plus the fact that they tell a story of some kind of dreadful massacre, is a bit unnerving. Right, Maggie?"

"You've pretty much summed it up." She stood, crossed her arms in front of her chest, and began pacing the room.

"Whoa, I didn't know it was this complicated." Joey stroked his chin as he considered the reverend's account. "How is Julia handling it?"

"Much better than I am," replied Maggie, stepping over Joey's outstretched feet as her pacing continued. "She's completely unruffled. Oh, and she thinks the girls might be us, or we might be the girls, or whatever."

Joey grabbed the arms of his chair as if preparing for blastoff. "Do you mean like from a former life?"

"Perhaps. But I've been brought up to believe this is the only life we have on this earth. One life. Here. No other chances to learn what we need to learn." She brushed one hand across the gigantic oak desk, scooting aside a blue glass paperweight in the process. "Isn't that right, Reverend Chamberlain?"

The church secretary, a short, plump woman with tightly permed gray hair, tapped at the narrow rectangular window in the door. The reverend opened it about four inches, said a few words to her, closed the door firmly, and sat back down. "Yes and no," he said.

Maggie twisted a strand of her hair. "Now you're sounding like me. Which is it?"

Joey sat back, hands clasped behind his head, smiling broadly as he crossed one long leg over the other.

Reverend Chamberlain went on. "Most Christians do interpret the Bible that way. But there are several references in the New Testament which, to me at least, suggest the possibility of reincarnation. I'm not entirely sure God wants us to know all the answers."

"But what else could it be?" Maggie demanded, her voice approaching the shrillness of an infuriated child.

The reverend's tone, as calm as always, encouraged Maggie to compose herself, at least outwardly.

"Here's another idea I've been considering since Claire called me last night," he said. "Suppose, if the timing was right and the need apparent, we could be given the knowledge of someone else's life in order to enrich our own, or possibly to assist theirs. What if all the forces of the universe, so to speak, came together to allow such a divine experience?"

"By 'forces of the universe,' I assume you include God," Maggie said.

"Certainly."

She walked over to the window to watch two young boys throw a football back and forth. "And what else?"

"May I respond to that?" Joey, completely at home by this point, poured himself a cup of coffee from the stainless steel pot in the corner.

Reverend Chamberlain swept his arm toward Joey. "Take it away, my friend."

"Maggie, think about it." Joey paused to slurp the hot coffee. "You and I have talked several times before today about the unique energy and behavior brought on by the full moon. It's when you have your dreams, and when I feel strangely empowered. And it's no secret that hospital staff, schoolteachers, and policemen often report unusual incidents during a full moon. But the moon isn't the only astronomical force out there. People joke about weird stuff taking place when the planets are aligned, but there is an element of truth to that."

"Are you trying to tell me it's something wacky like the 'Age of Aquarius'? That's absurd." Maggie ran her fingers through her hair in frustration. "And why me? Why Julia?"

"We'll address the why part in a minute," said Reverend Chamberlain.

"Back to the moon," Joey persisted. "There's an imaginary flat oval surface in space on which the earth travels. When the sun, Earth, and moon coincide in specific positions on that elliptical plane, we observe either a solar or lunar eclipse."

"The mysterious plane of the ecliptic you wanted to tell me about? Very interesting, but once again, what does that have to do with me?" Exhausted after the occurrences of the weekend, Maggie had no patience for a lecture on astronomy.

Reverend Chamberlain interrupted. "It seems like an analogy to the idea we just mentioned—certain forces lining up to permit an extraordinary occurrence. Like the hand of God arranging a small miracle for you to witness."

Joey went on. "What if, like the reverend said, certain people and events come together for a specific purpose? And does it really matter if we understand every aspect? It's what we do with the experience that makes it significant. I'm pretty sure you were the one who told me that a few years ago."

"Maybe." At the risk of hyperventilating, Maggie took one slow, deep breath after another. "So you're both saying Julia and I did not necessarily live the lives of the two girls in Scotland, but maybe we are being allowed, for whatever reason, to encounter them now? That somehow we've been given permission to glimpse a portion of their lives in parallel to our own?"

"Yes," the two men shouted together.

"I need to use the bathroom. I'll be right back." Maggie walked out of the office and closed the door, leaving her minister and her former student alone. She knew they would more than likely keep the discussion going until she returned.

What she really needed was time to think. In the restroom, she splashed water on her face, washed her hands thoroughly with the foamy pink soap from the dispenser, and stared into the mirror. After a full fifteen or sixteen minutes, she straightened the collar on her cream-colored blouse, blew her nose on a scratchy paper towel, and walked back down the hallway.

The two men halted in mid-sentence as the door creaked open.

"All right," she said as she reclaimed her seat. "Is it also feasible these memories have been carried through the genes of our ancestors? Could Julia and I be physically related to the girls, Rebeca and Gillian? What about that theory?"

"A viable supposition." Joey scrunched up his eyes, bobbing his head from side to side.

"It's something I hadn't really considered, but it definitely seems possible," Reverend Chamberlain said. "And it would make sense, since Julia is not your biological granddaughter. The girls in the dreams are friends, not relatives. Hmm ... very clever, Maggie."

Joey opened his arms wide and stretched upward. "No matter how you look at it, this is some form of synchronicity at its finest," he proclaimed.

Maggie rolled her eyes. "Am I now supposed to know what you mean by synchronicity?"

"It's Carl Jung's principle, wherein specific events in life are perceived as meaningful coincidences," Joey explained. "That's the short version, of course. I studied Jung in an undergraduate psych course."

"It also involves precise timing," added Reverend Chamberlain.

"So we have a couple of ideas to contemplate then," Maggie said, both amazed and relieved with the path this conversation had taken. "Easy enough to handle, I suppose. But what about the 'why me' part?"

"Only you and Julia can figure that out." Reverend Chamberlain stepped around his desk, standing next to Joey's chair.

"Terrific," Maggie said. "Swell. And just how are we supposed to do that?"

"We were figuring that out while you were in the bathroom," said Joey. He and the reverend, obviously staunch comrades in their new mission, glanced first at each other and then at Maggie.

"At the next full moon," began Revered Chamberlain, "why don't you and Julia pray together before you go to sleep? Ask for some explanation as to the reason for the story of these two girls being presented to you. Pose the question, 'What might we learn from the dreams?'"

"But, Maggie?" Joey scooted his chair closer.

"Yes?"

"The answer might be one you're not expecting. Since it's still unclear after so many years, I have a feeling you're in for a surprise. Make absolutely certain you're ready to hear the answer."

With that, the man of science followed the man of religion out the door.

"Hey, wait!" Maggie yelled after them. "Why did you really want to talk to me?"

Chapter 21

That evening, after her discussion with Joey and Reverend Chamberlain, Maggie called Julia. It seemed so simple now, this notion of using prayer and the scientific power of the full moon to direct the course of their dreams. Although they might have once considered such a measure bizarre, to Maggie and Julia it now appeared to be quite natural. They wondered why they hadn't thought of it before.

"I'm so excited, Gammy," Julia said. "This will be a really good thing for us."

Suddenly Maggie was happy. And it showed.

She was in such an extraordinarily good mood at school, the staff and students were drawn to her like children to the Pied Piper, delighted to be in her presence. Her contagious aura of tranquility attracted the teenagers especially, all of whom were on their perpetual adolescent carnival ride of fluctuating emotions and hormones. At lunchtime, the library filled with students studying for upcoming quizzes or exams. Maggie loved the casual conversation she had with them during this part of the day. Relaxed and confident, she asked what movies they'd seen recently or which rock bands were currently popular. A few girls asked her advice about parents and boyfriends. All conversations that Maggie had never been part of before. She felt young and hip, and exceptionally wise.

On day eleven of the countdown, a Sunday, the entire family accompanied Maggie to church, an event she took as a sign of better days to come. Claire was already there, just as she had been several weeks in a row. This time, however, she was waiting with Gina.

Smoothing out her black pants and adjusting the cowl neck of her hot pink sweater, Gina scooted next to Julia. "Hope it's all right if I give your church a try," she whispered.

Julia patted her hand. "It's cool."

Maggie didn't blink an eye when Reverend Chamberlain started talking about Biblical references to celestial bodies and their relevance within God's universal plan. After their conversation in his office, nothing surprised her anymore. Initially, she had experienced a moment of guilt over not confiding in Ross, Kellie, or Claire, and then rationalized they would only have too many distracting questions. Gina might understand, but she would have to be caught up on the whole scenario, and Maggie just didn't feel like explaining everything to her right now.

At the end of the service, Reverend Chamberlain abruptly materialized next to Maggie and led her off to a side doorway. His serious expression alarmed her. "Maggie, you look so preoccupied. How's everything going? Still feeling okay about our little talk?"

"Oh, everything's fine, just fine," she chirped, and darted away to look for Ross. Gina had him cornered by the water fountain.

"Gina's making chicken cacciatore tonight, honey," Ross said. "Want to go for dinner?"

Maggie couldn't resist the looks of anticipation on both Ross's and Gina's faces. They were too cute. "That will be fun. Looking forward to it."

Later that night, Ross suggested they invite Gina to their house next time. "You're a great cook as well, Maggie. We should reciprocate."

"Yes, I agree," said Maggie. "But let's wait for a little while." When Ross gave her a puzzled look, she added, "It's the usual spring madhouse at school and I'm pretty pooped."

"That's all right," he replied, satisfied. "I'll be out in the backyard with Spencer for a few minutes. Anything good on television tonight?"

"I'll look in a second." She picked up the remote and pushed the power button but headed down the hall toward the computer instead of waiting to see what was on. She hated the way she had become dependent on the damn thing, yet night after night she gave in willingly to the addictive impulse to check her e-mail.

As she sat there staring at the empty mailbox, a message came through. Joey.

Maggie,
My computer has been having issues (nice way of saying it crashed). The love/hate relationship I have with it is making me psycho. Otherwise, I'm fine.
When I saw you in the reverend's office a couple weeks ago, I meant to tell you my big news ... I'm getting married! Her name is Elena and she's beautiful & smart & puts up with all my weirdness.
Hey, you know I fully support what you and Julia are planning to do at the next full moon, but I'm somewhat worried about you all the same. Let me know how it goes. And may the force be with you ...
Joey

Well, well, thought Maggie. *Joey's getting married. And he's still cautioning me. Wouldn't any type of resolution for the reason behind these dreams be a good thing?*

Out of the mood now for a television show, which was bound to be silly and meaningless, she found it rather gratifying to march right up to the set and turn it off. See? Bringing an end to her turmoil should be just as easy as that.

Chapter 22

At first, neither Maggie nor Julia realized that the night of the next full moon also happened to be Julia's tenth birthday. Consequently, it turned out be a special day all on its own, with a celebratory dinner, chocolate ice cream cake, and presents. As usual, Julia downplayed her own birthday, insisting on only one present from everybody. The dinner and cake were fine, she said, but a bunch of money spent on extravagant gifts was totally unnecessary. The previous year she had asked for and received a nice set of classic novels. Maggie had given her many other books over the years, but it was *A Tree Grows in Brooklyn* that Julia read in a week, setting the others aside. This year, her single request was for a bookcase to house her growing collection.

After they polished off the chicken and dumplings dinner and Maggie had gone in search of candles, Julia pulled her mother aside to ask permission to spend the night at her grandparents' house. Still wary of what had come out at the family meeting a month ago, Kellie agreed with one condition. "Especially because it's your birthday," she told Julia, "you must make an extra effort to get along. Don't upset your grandma. Not tonight."

"You worry too much, Mother," Julia assured her. "I'm expecting tonight to be just perfect." And she scampered away like a squirrel headed for a secret cache of nuts.

Although they hadn't discussed this particular detail, Julia was not surprised when Maggie showed up at the door to the guest room at bedtime. "Mind if I join you?" she asked.

Julia wore the flannel pajamas with the red-vested penguins she kept at her grandparents'. She pulled back the covers. "I figured you might want to sleep with me."

Maggie crawled in. They lay side by side on their backs, covers up to their necks, arms resting next to each other.

"What about Grandpa?" asked Julia, adjusting her pillow.

"He'll never miss me," Maggie replied. "I told him I wasn't sleepy yet and that I was going to make sure the birthday girl was set for the night. He's probably snoring already."

Julia turned out the lamp. They giggled nervously for a moment before making a conscious effort to relax.

"Are you ready, sweetheart?" Maggie asked.

"I think so. We're doing the right thing, you know."

"We're doing the only thing we can do."

"Why don't you start, Gammy?"

Maggie collected her thoughts for a moment. "Dear God, we ask for your divine guidance in our dreams tonight."

Julia continued, "We pray for the moon's light to help us see Gillian and Rebeca more clearly."

"Please show us how their lives relate to ours." Maggie's heart beat a teeny bit faster.

"And let this dream bring us wisdom and peace. Well, at least eventually," Julia added.

"Amen," they whispered together. The clock said 10:34. They closed their eyes.

"No, no, no!" Screams come from all directions. Too familiar. Like the night of the killings.

"Mrs. Saunders, be ye absolutely certain?" Rebeca asks. *Unbelievable. Must be a lie.*

"Sweetheart, I'm afraid 'tis true. 'Twas Clan Campbell who did the killin'. Direct orders from King William himself. I didna want to believe it either, but I saw it with me own eyes, I did. And the reports comin' from Edinburgh say just that. I thought it best to wait 'til we arrived safe in Inverness to tell ye." *Mrs. Saunders wipes an eye.*

"But the Campbells stayed with us. They ate with us, slept in our beds. They were our friends," says Gillian.

Everyone quiet now, wondering. How could they do it?

"Only pretended to be our friends, me dear, and a grand job they did too. 'Twas part o' their plan—gain our trust and then betray us in the very worst way." *Mrs. Saunders runs her fingers through her bushy hair.* "King William didna appreciate Clan MacDonald's hesitation in taking the oath o' allegiance, I guess."

"How many died?" *a tall, thin girl whispers.*

"I been told they murdered thirty-eight men. But after they set the houses on fire, another forty died tryin' to escape in the snow, mostly women and children. Will never be forgotten, what the Campbells did in Glencoe. Never forgotten, nor forgiven."

Girls crying. Sobbing. Holding each other. Gillian and Rebeca look around, unbelieving.

"Rebeca, come with me a minute." *Mrs. Saunders takes her hand. Leads her to a back room. Church is dark, chilly. Musty smell.*

"Lass, I know ye be a Campbell. But I don't know for certain if your da was part o' the madness. I canna believe he would bring you along if he knew o' the plans."

Rebeca hangs her head. Hands tremble. Tremendous fear inside. What would Mrs. Saunders do to her?

"What I mean to say is, ye shouldna feel badly. Oh no. Young lasses canna be blamed for the sins o' their fathers. Ye canna take on any guilt by this horrible act, do ye hear me?" *Mrs. Saunders reaches over. Lifts her chin.*

"But what shall I do? How can I think o' me da now after this? And me mam! Does she know? I want to see her!"

"'Tis best ye not try to see her now, lassie. 'Tis too dangerous yet. Ye be needin' to cut your hair short too. Didna want anyone to recognize ye as the girl who came to the highlands with a Campbell. Best if ye try to start new."

"But what shall become o' me? Can I still learn to be a governess? Can I go to the school with Gillian?" Voice frantic. Entire body shaking now.

"Ay, ye may do just that, Rebeca. But when 'tis time to go off to take care o' the bairns, ye will be on your own. No one can promise ye will see young Gillian again after that." Mrs. Saunders hugs her. "I'll leave ye for a minute to take this all in."

Rebeca cries. Can't stop. Gulping, sobbing.

Gillian comes in through doorway. Hugs Rebeca tight. "All right, now, it be all right," she says.

"Oh, Gilli, how can it ever be all right? 'Twas me own clan who murdered the Maclains! And now I must pretend to be a Maclain, not a Campbell. Me hair—she wants to cut me bonnie red hair."

"I wish I could have your hair for me own. I'd trade ye any day."

"And I could have yours. If I had your brown hair, I wouldna stand out so much." Rebeca starts to cry. "She says I can be with ye until the schoolin's done, but then I might not see ye again, Gillian. Oh God, I can barely stand to think about it."

Girls sit together on stone bench, sniffling.

"Rebeca, I do not blame ye for what the men did. Ye best know that, and not ever forget it. Ye always be me finest friend no matter where our lives may take us. Ay, we will find each other again somehow."

Rebeca wipes eyes. Looks at Gillian.

"Do ye believe me?" says Gillian.

"Ay. I must believe or surely daft I'll go."

Maggie stared at the bedroom ceiling. An enormous and brilliant amber moon shone like a beacon directly onto the bed, a search light locating its target. Her heart slowly crumbled under the weight of the knowledge she had longed for and now wished would disappear. The meaning of this dream, the truth she'd been certain would set her free, gradually sank into a place so deep inside her, she wondered if she'd ever be able to bring it back up to the surface. All she could think of were Joey's words of warning.

"Gammy?"

Julia's voice startled her. Maggie turned her head to find her granddaughter—she was still her granddaughter, wasn't she?—poised at the window, her young face, curly hair, and penguin pajamas shimmering like that of a glow-in-the-dark doll. Without speaking, Maggie compelled her legs to walk toward her.

"This explains a lot, doesn't it?" asked Julia, calmly inspecting the brilliant ring of light circling the moon.

Maggie's head felt like it was underwater. If she opened her mouth, only indecipherable bubbles would emerge.

Julia went on. "What heartache those girls endured. Well, the entire village, for that matter."

Still nothing from Maggie.

Julia waited another minute. "Gammy, we could choose to let this go now. It would be okay with me to agree to bring this to a close right here tonight and go on with our lives. Is that what you want to do?"

The top of Maggie's head barely broke the surface of the water. She tilted her face up so her nose and mouth could feel the air. Gasping, she watched the first bubble burst. "The redhead wasn't like you after all, was she?"

Julia wisely, serenely answered, "I tried to tell you that at the family meeting."

"How did you know then?"

"Just the way Rebeca was so uneasy and afraid about what was happening, and Gillian accepted all the changes as they came along. The girls were basically experiencing the same thing, but the way they handled it was vastly different. Sounds familiar, doesn't it, Gammy?" Julia held back a tiny smile. "Plus, there was the flute."

Oh, the flute. Of course. Yet again astounded by this intuitive girl, Maggie began to return to reality. Her voice rose to a pitch not unlike that of a faulty microphone. "But don't you see?" she squealed unevenly. "If we truly are those girls, or somehow have memories of them, or if they're trying to identify with us, or whatever is happening here—then I'm a Campbell. I'm part of the reason behind that unspeakable night!"

Maggie began crying.

Julia, apparently helpless to extend comfort in any of the traditional methods, ventured beyond customary logic and everyday reasoning. She gently touched her grandmother's face and said, "Rebeca, I do not blame you."

Part 3

Three things cannot be long hidden:
the sun, the moon, and the truth.

—Siddhartha Gautama

Chapter 23

That September, Maggie made up her mind to retire at the end of the school year. As usual, she had gone into the library a couple of weeks early to make sure it was clean, orderly, and ready to go for the opening day. Some librarians would have just shown up on the first day with the students, called it good, and started working. But Maggie had new books to process that had arrived over the summer, classroom textbooks shipped from the bindery to pass back to teachers, fresh bulletin boards to put up, plants to return from home, and a summer's worth of mail to sort through. Returning students expected to be able to walk over to the stacks and find a book exactly where it should be or plop their research materials next to a computer devoid of grimy fingerprints. Maggie wouldn't dream of disappointing them.

Besides, if she kept her life normal and routine, then maybe, just maybe, the dreams and all the issues they brought with them would magically disappear.

In the middle of measuring the aquamarine butcher paper for the book recommendation board, she was suddenly struck with the realization of how many times she'd taken care of these tasks. She'd started teaching right out of college when she was barely twenty-two; after this school year ended, she would turn sixty. Jesus God. That was long enough. She would make this her best year ever, go over and above even her own expectations, and then quietly leave to make way for some idealistic newcomer full of energy and enthusiasm. It was time.

Maggie told Claire before she told anyone else. Claire was only fifty-six but had been talking about retirement since she was fifty. "What will you do with all your extra time?" she asked, as if she had never considered the numerous possibilities herself.

"Lots of things," replied Maggie. "You know, read all the books I've never gotten around to, redecorate the guest room, put together family photo albums for Kellie and Julia. Stuff like that. I could volunteer at the public library or deliver Meals on Wheels if I wanted. After tax season next spring, Ross is thinking of retiring too. We want to travel. We've never ventured very far from Summerhill. I'll be so busy, I'm sure I won't know how I ever managed to go to school every day."

"Maggie?"

"What?"

"Does this have anything to do with Julia and the dreams and everything?" Claire moved directly in front of her friend and watched her face carefully.

Maggie met Claire's gaze before turning slightly to the left. "Maybe it does, maybe it doesn't," she said. "So what? I've worked more than enough years to get good benefits, it feels like the right thing to do, and I'm going to do it. Period."

Obviously shocked by her friend's determined statement, Claire backed off.

What Maggie was unwilling to tell Claire was, yes, the dreams underlay all of her decisions. The revelatory dream on the night of Julia's birthday had stopped her cold. She knew it was meant to help her figure something out about herself, but it was overwhelming, confusing, and downright weird. She longed to simplify her daily life, relax, and allow the dreams to unfold.

Easier said than done, of course. In the meantime, she had found a perfect way to keep her nights undisturbed.

Ross's reaction to her retirement announcement was slightly different. His first question surprised her. "Won't you miss the students?" he said.

"Well, yes, I will," she answered. "But I can't keep going until I'm eighty or ninety, just to be around them. I admit it's difficult to get to know them like I do and then just leave. But they leave *me* every year when they graduate. It's part of the process, whether I like it or not."

"Where shall we go first?"

"You mean as in a vacation?" she asked.

"Yes, a vacation. I'd love to go back east and visit the Civil War battlefields. Or Florida. We could go to Disney World and then ride one of those hovercraft things over the Everglades. Italy would be fun. Think how great it would be to have a plate of spaghetti in Florence or float on a gondola in Venice."

"Ross, how about the place we've talked about forever?"

They looked at each other, smiling.

"We could take Kellie and Julia with us," she continued.

"Get yourself a hula skirt, Mag! Hawaii, here we come. I'll call a travel agent tomorrow so we can start looking at itineraries."

At the end of the first semester, Maggie's decision started to sink in. She had filled out the required paperwork, so there was no turning back now. But as she wrote purchase orders for the remainder of her library funds, something she always did midyear just in case there was a surprise budget freeze, she realized she would actually miss the tedious task of reviewing, selecting, and purchasing new books. The process took hours, at least for the meticulous Maggie. She carefully researched every title, checked and double-checked, and finally ordered with a great deal of love and pride. She knew any one of the books might change the life of a student, in ways she couldn't begin to imagine.

Maggie's student aides were fantastic. Or maybe she just felt an extraordinary appreciation for them this particular year. All she knew was that the three of them were bright, funny, hardworking, and as different from one another as if they had been born in foreign countries around the world and then adopted by one mother—Maggie.

Angela was tall, blonde, and strikingly beautiful. She would surely be valedictorian in June, would go on to medical school to study pediatrics, and eventually marry a handsome, sensitive, successful man, not unlike her current boyfriend, Tom Lassiter. Angela had won the speech and declamation contest for the third year in a row and had acted the lead of Glorianna in the fall production of *The Mouse That Roared*. She helped Maggie keep the library in perfect order, right down to alphabetizing titles within specific authors. In the midst of all this perfection, Angela managed to maintain a genuine compassion and sincere interest for everyone around her, including her teachers. Her attitude and demeanor were so mature, Maggie had to catch herself to keep from treating her as an adult friend.

Sophie, a petite Korean girl living with her grandmother, only needed to be told something one time and she had it. Plus, she recognized what should be done each day and simply did it without being asked. In November, Sophie had opened up to Maggie, explaining her father had disappeared six years before, her mother was a meth addict living on the streets, and she'd probably never see either of them again. She admired her grandmother for taking on the challenge of raising her, while both of them mourned the slow demise of her mother. Eager to please, she appreciated every ounce of attention and kindness Maggie brought her way. Maggie looked for ways of boosting her self-esteem in an attempt to shorten the years of therapy she might need later in life to deal with her messed-up adolescence.

And then there was Connor. Connor, with the biweekly change of hair color, all-black wardrobe, and body piercings that Maggie was certain he'd sincerely regret later. Connor was the gentle intellectual, the wistfully romantic boy who regularly contemplated extinct birds and famine in Africa. Maggie expected to read in twenty years how his private laboratory had developed a medicine that would not only fight cancer, but also would encourage peaceful, generous personalities. On top of all that, he was funny.

"Mrs. MacKenzie?" he asked one day. He adjusted the ring in his left eyebrow before stuffing his Peace Corps brochure into his backpack.

"Yes."

"Do you ever listen to Jeff Foxworthy? Man, that dude is an absolute riot."

Maggie wondered what Mr. Foxworthy's reaction would be to this very un-Southern, un-redneck fan of his. "Connor, it never ceases to amaze me that you and I share the same sense of humor."

He wheeled the book cart over toward the reference section. "It shouldn't be a surprise, Mrs. M.," he called over his shoulder. "Most of the world is so depressing, I have to find every way possible to generate a good laugh."

Maggie smiled and shook her head. How could she leave this boy, still just an impressionable sophomore, at the end of the school year?

Before Maggie knew it, it was mid-May. She met Claire on a clear, sunny Saturday at the Starbucks on Spruce and Third. Even though the morning air was cool and breezy, it held the promise of summer, lifting Maggie's spirits about her impending retirement. Already waiting with her tall iced mocha, Claire waved her over.

Maggie ordered a decaf of the day and sat down. "All ready to wrap up another year?" she asked.

"I suppose so. It'll come whether I'm ready or not," said Claire. "How are you getting along? Still feeling like you're doing the right thing?"

"Most of the time. To be honest, there are days when I just can't picture not being at school. But having time to travel and do other things with Ross sounds more appealing every day. We have our Hawaiian trip already booked for next winter. Kellie and Julia can hardly wait."

Claire looked out the window at a gray and white cat totally zonked out on the warm sidewalk. "That does sound relaxing," she said. "Well, I envy you. I'm thinking I'll stick it out another three years or so."

They drank their coffee, watching the cat stretch its back, wash its face, and saunter away in search of another napping place.

"How's Jack?" Maggie asked.

"Okay. He hurt his back last week trying to do some work under the car. Now it's killing him to rest like the doctor ordered."

"What about Bill?"

"He's fine. He and Evelyn invited us over for dinner last month. She fixed the best beef stew and biscuits. They seem pretty happy."

"She must be an exceptional woman to accept your friendship with Bill, considering, you know, all that happened," Maggie said.

Claire sipped her mocha. "Yes, I know. It's fascinating how things seem to work out sometimes, isn't it? I truly value Bill's friendship, but he and I were never meant to be anything more than friends. I love it when everything becomes clear."

Maggie didn't answer. Her coffee had grown cold, but she couldn't bring herself to give it up.

"Speaking of becoming clear, have you had any interesting dreams lately?" Claire seemed annoyed that she actually had to ask.

"No. Not for a while. I suppose they're over for now."

"You don't say," muttered Claire.

The rest of Maggie's Saturday went perfectly. Following her visit with Claire, she stopped at the dry cleaners to pick up the dress she would wear to the retirement dinner next month, filled her gas tank, got groceries at the market on Lincoln Avenue, and went home to make herself a sandwich. She spent the afternoon typing a detailed list of her many duties as Summerhill High's librarian. No one had been hired yet to fill the position, but whoever the new librarian was, he or she would certainly appreciate having everything written up. When she had covered issues from where to order magazine covers and date-due slips, to how to account for the days the school would be closed in the circulation software program, she printed the list and shut down her computer, feeling confident in sharing her thirty-eight years of experience. Hopefully, her replacement would be capable of dealing with Joan Dixon's habit of forgetting to bring her classes down on the days she'd signed up, would learn how to keep the custodians happy and willing to do a few extras for the library, and wouldn't take it personally when Harry Leftwich snuck in the occasional comment that the librarian had the easiest job in the school. It was impossible for Maggie to fully prepare anyone for the daily politics of the educational system.

After dinner, she put on a light sweater and joined Ross outside on the deck with a glass of lemonade. Spencer and Cleo sat side by side in the far corner, as if looking over their property, something they had started doing a few years before. These days they acted like an old married couple who was so used to each other, they chose to ignore any previous conflicts.

Spencer, almost twelve, shifted slightly from hip to hip, unconsciously relieving his painful arthritis. The daily dose of Rimadyl helped, but clearly he still suffered. Typical of his breed, he never complained. Instead he sought out and focused on each opportunity for happiness. This time of year offered him a host of possibilities—rolling on his back in the cool grass, chasing his red ball, watching Ross plant the cucumbers, smelling the lilac bush. Cleo, a year older than her big hairy brother, seemed unchanged from five years earlier. She ate only what she needed, slept most of the day, pounced on bugs and fluttering leaves, and cautiously investigated any new piece of furniture. Thank goodness she had lost her desire to bring home dead mice.

Ross had completed his final tax season the month before and could hardly wait to clean out his desk and devote the entire summer to his garden. "Happy?" he asked.

Maggie rattled the ice in her glass and reached over for his hand. "Why? Have any ideas on how to make me happier?" she joked.

"Hmm … Now that you mention it, I can think of a couple." He grinned. "Seriously, Maggie, besides the traveling we have planned, is there anything else you still want to do with your life?"

She chose her words carefully. "I'd have to give it some thought, I suppose. What about you, honey?"

Ross looked like a man who'd just been told the universal secret of life. "Look around," he said. "I have everything I could ever want. I do wish more than anything, though, that I could help you figure out why you're having those dreams."

They sat in the silence of the moment as the sun disappeared behind Mt. Creston and the moon peeked around the maple tree.

"Coming up to bed?" Ross invited. Spencer and Cleo, evidently thinking he was talking to them, raced for the screen door.

"I'll be right behind you," said Maggie.

She made sure all the doors were locked, turned on the dishwasher, transferred a package of ground turkey from the freezer to the refrigerator, and formed a mental list with each step up the stairs. Wash face, apply moisturizer, brush teeth, pee, wash hands, have sex with Ross, pee again, wash hands, take sleeping pill.

Ah, the little blue sleeping pill, her guarantee for yet another peaceful, dreamless night.

Chapter 24

Maggie had no reason to dwell on turning sixty. Although she had reluctantly given in to having her hair colored to cover the gray and didn't always have as much energy as she used to, she was healthy and reasonably happy. Even the tiny wrinkles around her eyes and the extra ten pounds she'd put on didn't really bother her. Since she had been a student, a teacher, or a librarian almost her entire life, her June birthday usually took a backseat to the last day of school. Ross had turned sixty the year before, and they'd celebrated with the customary dinner at a fancy restaurant. Cake and presents followed at home. She looked forward to the same simple tradition.

Her career came to a calm and respectful close, just as she had anticipated, with no fanfare or elaborate to-do. As always, she gave her three student aides an end-of-the-year gift to show her appreciation for their hard work. Although she often purchased gift cards from the local bookstore, this time her mind was on blue oceans and sandy beaches, so she bought fluffy, bright beach towels instead. Sophie blurted out, "Mrs. MacKenzie, this will be so much better than the old bath towel I usually have to use when I go to the lake." Maggie hugged them all, as well as the many students who stopped by to see her. One student, a chubby boy with thick glasses and a pocket protector, whom Maggie had guided toward the fantasy stories of Diane Wynn-Jones and Phillip Pullman, was too choked up to speak. Eventually, he just shook his head, waved his arms up and down, and ran out of the library.

On her last day of work, with students sleeping in at home or already at their summer jobs, she straightened each book, pulling each one forward so every title was visible and accessible, shelf after shelf, like newly trimmed hedge rows. She turned in her keys and the remainder of her late-fine money to Lois in the office, lingering for a few minutes to chat about summer plans. Several teachers and both principals stopped by to repeat their good wishes, all of them making a point of telling her how many more years they had to work before they would be lucky enough to retire. She cleaned out her computer, deleting e-mail files and removing folders of projects too personal to be used by anyone other than she. The new librarian, now known to be a thirty-six-year-old former eighth-grade English teacher from Bellingham, would undoubtedly bring new ideas and a style of her own. But Maggie's stack of impeccable instructions lay on the desk, just in case.

Although most teachers had finished their report cards, piled up their textbooks, and zoomed out of the parking lot by 1:30, Maggie stayed on, puttering around like she was expecting company. Finally at 3:10, when she couldn't think of a single thing left to do, she gathered up her photos of Ross, Kellie, and Julia, along with her insulated blue lunch bag, and walked out, ready to begin the next chapter in her life.

That was Wednesday.

By the time her birthday came around on Friday, Maggie was already at a loss for a way to keep occupied. The house was spotless, she didn't feel like starting one of the books in her bedside stash, and the summer ahead had a totally different feel to it.

No matter what the weather, she was on a permanent, endless summer vacation from now on. She felt like Alice arriving in Wonderland. The world was strange and challenging.

She had been so busy getting every detail in order at school, she hadn't talked to Ross much about her birthday. She'd been thinking she might like to go out for a family dinner at Bambino's, where the baked ziti was excellent and the crusty bread dripped with just the right amount of butter and garlic. When she mentioned it to Ross over coffee that morning, however, he had a different idea.

"Kellie wants to have us over for dinner at her house," he said, peering at the classified ads. "I meant to bring it up yesterday and forgot."

"Terrific," Maggie said. Not wanting to show even a slight sign of disappointment, she purposely didn't ask what Kellie was fixing. Kellie was a terrific cook, and Maggie was sure someone would think of a birthday cake. It would be fine.

Ross insisted she take it easy all day. No cleaning, no working, no fussing around of any kind. Since she had reached a standstill in general activity anyway, it was easy to honor his request. She tried calling Claire, left a message, sent off an e-mail to Joey, and finally turned on the DVD player to watch *Grease*, one of her favorite movies. *That John Travolta is about the cutest thing ever,* she thought and found herself rewinding the Greased Lightning car scene three times.

At 6:00, they pulled up to Kellie's house, after what Maggie deemed one of the longest, but most relaxing, days of her life. Ross turned to her and said, "Ready?"

Ready to have dinner at their daughter's house? Ross was not quite himself, but then his day had been the opposite of Maggie's. Although he'd found errand after errand to run, he'd brought home only a small package of new screwdrivers. Maggie saw no point in asking him what his current project was. She knew he would mull it over in his mind for a few days before he was willing to talk about it. Evidently he'd also managed to stop for a haircut. He'd showered and now sported the fresh-faced, well-scrubbed look of a young boy on his way to visit an elderly aunt.

Ross knocked once on Kellie's front door, and then just opened it, urging Maggie to go in ahead of him.

She froze as a chorus of "Surprise!" almost forced her back onto the porch. At first she thought she and Ross had somehow stepped into the wrong house, as impossible as that might be. But the faces slowly started to come into focus—Kellie, Julia, Claire and Jack, Bill and Evelyn Guthrie, Angela, Sophie, Connor, the entire language arts department, Lois, the school's office manager, Gina from next door, and oh my god, there was Joey Martinez. Her knees buckled as she looked at her delighted husband, and she grabbed his arm to steady herself.

"Happy Birthday, Mag," he said.

In the state of shock known only to those who have come upon the utterly unexpected, Maggie allowed Julia to lead her to the back patio, where there was a spread of lasagna, baked ziti, chicken parmesan, green salad, and garlic bread. A gigantic sheet cake with "Happy 60th Birthday, Maggie" spelled out with miniature books sat among balloons on a side table. When at last she felt like her mouth might have a chance at working properly, she asked Kellie if she had done all this herself.

"You're kidding, right?" she said. "I've been too busy trying to keep Dad from spilling the beans! It's Bambino's catering service."

Maggie was stunned. How could she not have known? She longed to think through the particulars of the last couple of weeks to figure out what signs she could possibly have missed, but she would apparently need to wait. Joey stood in front of her, beaming, a beautiful young woman and a curly-headed baby boy at his side.

"Maggie, this is my wife, Elena, and our son, Henry."

Maggie made a conscious effort to glide back into reality. She took a second look, saying, "I can't believe it."

Joey laughed. "What? Us or the surprise party?"

"Both!"

Somehow she moved through the fog of the next few hours, trying to visit with everyone, barely tasting the dinner she'd been craving all day. Claire, Jack, and Gina were the last guests to leave. Kellie wrapped up all the leftovers, swept the kitchen floor, and lit the citronella candle on the patio table. Ross carried one last trash bag to the garage and then joined his three girls outside. The summer solstice would occur in less than a week, and the half moon shone like a gigantic lemon wedge.

"You're not mad, are you?" he asked.

"Are you crazy?" Maggie replied. "Why would I be mad? This was an unbelievably magnificent surprise. Huge emphasis on surprise, of course."

"Well, you told us in no uncertain terms you didn't want a big deal made out of your retirement. But ..." He chuckled. "You didn't say anything about your birthday."

Maggie loved this man more than she could express. She was deeply touched he'd done this for her. "Ross, it was perfect. I still don't know how you managed to keep it a secret, but you really pulled it off. You thought of everything. My favorite food, my favorite people, even the cake was unforgettable. You are magnificent, all three of you. Thank you for the best birthday I've ever had."

Julia had remained relatively quiet all evening, but now she sat down on the edge of the lounger next to Maggie's chair, slipped off her pink flip-flops, and pulled away her elastic hair tie. Her reddish curls fell around her bare shoulders like mounds of ribbon adorning a festive package. "Gammy, we love you very much. Here's to all your days ahead. May they be filled with deep meaning and happiness."

"Well put," said Kellie

"To all the days ahead," said Ross.

A cool breeze suddenly whirled around them, sending a peculiar chill down their bare limbs.

Chapter 25

Except for the collection of birthday cards Ross had gathered up before they left Kellie's house the night before, Maggie would have dismissed the entire evening as a moment of fanciful illusion. But the next morning the cards were on the kitchen counter, as authentic as the granite beneath them. Maggie poured herself a cup of coffee, made two pieces of toast smeared with Gina's strawberry jam, and sat down to reread the stack of good wishes. She loved Julia's the most. The card itself was sweet, but she'd taken the time to write a lengthy note about how she loved being the granddaughter of a woman so wise, sensitive, loving, and brave. Brave? Maggie didn't often feel brave. She did, of course, feel very close to Julia and knew their relationship was like no other between a grandmother and granddaughter, biological or otherwise.

Ross and Maggie had recalled every detail of the party while getting ready for bed the night before—the food, the friends, the laughing, the overall wonderfulness of the entire evening. Maggie marveled over how Ross had put the party together so beautifully, so secretly, and felt utterly humbled. She would remember the night for the rest of her life, and told him so as they wrapped their arms around each other in bed.

"How are you feeling today, honey?" Ross asked. Spencer sat at attention by the back door, ball in his mouth, staring at Ross. He had watched his master put on his gardening shoes and could hardly wait for some outdoor fun.

"Absolutely fabulous. I can't describe it, really. You gave me a precious gift last night, sweetheart. Thank you again. How about you?"

Ross hesitated. "Honestly, a little off, if you know what I mean. I'm probably just let down from all the excitement of yesterday, kind of like the day after Christmas. I'll be fine after I dig in the dirt for a while. That always puts things in perspective for me."

"Well, don't stay out too long. It's supposed to get pretty hot today," Maggie warned him.

"Yes, dear," Ross joked. They both knew he'd come in when he had finished what he wanted to do in the garden and not before, sweat more than likely running down his face and back. "Oh, Maggie?"

"Yes?"

"I had a really pleasant dream about your parents last night."

"You did?"

"Yeah, it was nice. They both looked great and wanted me to go for a ride with them in this beautiful car." Ross scratched his head. "Your mom got in the backseat with me."

Maggie thought it unusual for Ross to actually remember one of his dreams, and especially curious he would dream about her parents instead of his own. But she only smiled at her husband. "I love you so much."

"And I love you more."

Maggie showered, put on a pair of sky blue shorts and a white T-shirt with blue embroidered cornflowers around the neckline, and called Claire. No answer. She dialed Kellie's number. No answer there either, so she left a long message about the amazing party, saying she hoped Kellie and Julia would have time to stop by that day so she could thank them more in person. "Sixty is turning out to be a pretty good thing," she said.

Finally, with no one to talk to and Ross working in the garden, she left to go pick up a few groceries. She knew the store by heart, hummed her way up and down every aisle, and returned home before lunchtime. After unpacking the chicken and fish, cleaning the produce for the week, and tossing the plastic bags in the recycling bin, she decided to convince Ross to come in for a sandwich and a glass of milk.

Spencer barked from across the yard. *Ross must not be throwing the ball often enough,* thought Maggie. But then Spencer barked again, and this time it came from the other side of the sliding door.

"Spencer? What's the matter, boy?" Spencer wore the most distressed look she had ever seen on a dog's face. Whining incessantly, he looked toward the garden and then back at Maggie. Ross was still there, leaning over the rototiller.

Maggie instinctively grabbed the cordless phone before following Spencer out to the garden, as if her only mission was to save Ross a trip to the house for a call.

But there would be no more calls for Ross MacKenzie. His upper body rested on the handles of the red rototiller he had used for the last fifteen years, its blades digging farther and farther into the softened soil. He was gone. His funny feeling earlier had apparently mushroomed into something major. His eyes were open, blank, an indication that the body he had occupied for over sixty years was now empty. Maggie reached over and turned off the tiller. Spencer uttered a combination of whimper and mournful howl, while Maggie lifted her husband from underneath his shoulders. As gently as she could, she laid his body down between the tomatoes and green beans, with his head resting on the edge of the lawn.

Spencer stretched out beside him, one dirty paw on his master's chest. The faithful dog's long sigh echoed the deep sorrow and frightening pain Maggie knew he must be feeling.

She remembered the phone and dialed 911. A nice man walked her through the steps she needed to take, checking Ross's pulse, watching for a rise in his chest or a whisper of a breath. Yes, she said, she knew CPR from training at school. She repeated their address, making sure to say her blue Subaru was in the driveway, and describing the trail of Ross's rosebushes that would lead the paramedics to the backyard, where she would be waiting. "And hurry," she said.

Push, push, push, push, push … Breathe, breathe. Push, push, push, push … Twenty-nine, thirty. Breathe, breathe. *Come on, Ross, come on.* Maggie pressed on his chest and blew air into his mouth for what seemed like an eternity, all the while knowing it was too late.

The sirens came from around the corner. Should she call Kellie now, or wait until the emergency people announced the official verdict? How could she bring herself to say the words out loud to Kellie and Julia? Would the ability to say the words be the deciding factor as to whether this astonishing event had truly happened? If she couldn't verbalize it, would that mean this was just one of those frustrating, nonsensical dreams, and she would jerk awake in a minute?

Maggie closed Ross's eyes and lovingly kissed each lid. She could do nothing else, except sit in the garden next to her husband and dog, unbelieving. She consciously looked all around her, up in the sky and over the neighborhood. Was he nearby watching her? Couldn't he show himself to her, just to verify that this was really happening? But Maggie saw only a cottony cloud similar to the hundreds she'd seen all week. How could the clouds not even notice or care what had just taken place?

She caught movement at the deck's sliding glass door, the same door she'd walked through just a few minutes prior—before she knew that her whole world had changed forever. Gina was bustling toward her with both Kellie and Julia right behind. All three shared an expression of overwhelming panic, but Gina was clearly the one in charge.

"I called them," she shouted across the yard. "I called them as soon as I saw out my window."

Paramedics and their equipment seemed to be everywhere. Gina gathered Maggie, Kellie, Julia, and Spencer back toward the maple tree. The two men and one woman knelt over Ross and poked, prodded, measured, felt, turned, and listened, until they finally stood up in unison, turned to the pale and trembling group under the tree, and shook their heads. No, they indicated, this man would not be returning to his rototiller or his dog or his family.

"We're so very sorry," the woman said. "It looks like a quick heart attack. We don't think he suffered at all."

Spencer apparently took the tone of the woman's voice to mean something comforting. His face relaxed slightly as he looked to Maggie for further consolation. She leaned over to put her arms around the big golden dog and found herself hugging him fiercely, as if that might possibly bring Ross to his feet. Instead, the tears poured endlessly out of her like the display of a fountain that had just been repaired. It was all Kellie and Julia needed to release their own sorrow. They joined Maggie on the grass, sobbing and stroking Spencer. The dog had given up all hope of any good news, and, in bewilderment, surrendered himself to these females. Remaining upright, Gina patted heads and murmured, "There, there."

Gina stayed on at the MacKenzie house long after the paramedics, ambulance, and funeral home car had departed. With just one trip next door to pick up a few ingredients from her refrigerator, she somehow threw together a delicious meal of Caesar salad, grilled chicken breasts, and hot sourdough bread. The trick would be to get everyone to come to the table.

Maggie sat stiffly in her chair, Cleo on her lap and Spencer on the floor by her feet. Her white T-shirt was stained with dirt, dog hair, and smears of mascara, but she barely noticed. Kellie and Julia alternately cuddled and reached for tissues together on the loveseat.

Finally Kellie spoke. "Mom, what can we do for you? I want to make sure you're going to be all right."

Maggie willed her mouth to open. She startled even herself with such a sensible response. "Honey, we'll get through this together. I think we're in too much shock right now to plan too far into the future, don't you? It's so unbelievable. One minute he was here and the next minute he wasn't."

Spencer moaned fretfully. His tail gave one big thump before he plopped his head back down on Maggie's shoe.

"It's definitely weird," said Julia, reaching for another tissue to dab her eyes. "But Grandpa will always be with us. He's just in another dimension we can't see yet. He'll be waiting for us when it's our turn to cross over."

They stared at Julia, amazed at her voice of reason and wisdom. This was Julia, even in sorrow.

Maggie brought them back to the practical. "I guess we need to talk about arrangements. Do we want to have a service for him?"

"Yes." No one hesitated with her answer, including Gina. In fact, she took that opportunity to lead them to the kitchen table. "We can discuss this over dinner," she said.

They realized how hungry they had become, and once the eating began, so did their ideas for the next few days. Ross had wanted to be cremated, with his remains stored at Peaceful View Cemetery, where he and Maggie purchased a spot ten years earlier. One decision taken care of. Julia offered to gather up pictures of Ross, from babyhood to the present, and create a video chronicle of his life. She had just learned in her computer class how to edit the pictures and add music, and promised to make it "cool but meaningful." Kellie said she would take care of the food if

Maggie would let her know how many people to expect. And Maggie would call the funeral home to confirm a date and time.

Plates were cleared, and everyone felt better about having something to do for the next few days. They would put together a memorable tribute to their wonderful Ross. After hugging, kissing, and crying a few minutes more, one by one they left Maggie alone.

Gina hesitated at the door. "I'd be glad to stay if you want some company," she said.

"Thanks, but I'd better start getting used to being by myself in the house."

"Okay, then. I'll call you tomorrow."

Maggie locked the door after her, started the dishwasher, turned out the lights, and headed upstairs to the empty bedroom. *Oh God, Ross. How will I survive without you?*

Spencer and Cleo followed at Maggie's heels, anxious to put an end to this confusing day. Maggie shortened her usual bedtime routine by merely washing her face, brushing her teeth, and climbing into bed. Cleo hopped on top of the covers, Spencer plunked down on the floor beside Maggie, and the three of them closed their eyes, falling asleep immediately.

The blue sleeping pills sat in the medicine cabinet, untouched and forgotten.

Chapter 26

"Thanks for being here," Maggie said as Claire and Jack finally pulled themselves away. They had hugged her so long and tight, she'd known it was as much for them as for her.

"It was beautiful." Claire wiped her eyes, smearing even more makeup. "And everyone had such great stories to tell. Ross would've loved it."

Jack frowned. "I just don't know if I can get used to not having him around."

Ross's accountant friends were gathered around the long table that displayed the same pictures Julia had used in the video—Ross as a boy, Ross graduating from high school, Ross holding baby Kellie, Ross and Maggie's wedding picture, Ross with Julia on his lap, Ross pruning his roses, Ross in the backyard with Spencer, Ross smiling next to the Christmas tree. His life was exhibited in the same orderly manner as lessons in a textbook. And now the course was over, all the lessons learned.

"How will I know you're all right?" Claire asked Maggie.

"I will be. I promise," said Maggie. "I don't expect it to be easy, but I'll figure out a way to handle it."

"I'm going to call you all the time, you know. I want you to talk or cry or get mad or complain or whatever else you feel like doing."

Maggie embraced her friend. "Thank you for being you, Claire. I know you'll be there for me just like you've always been."

Ross's two brothers, Will and Charlie, were already beginning the tasks necessary to put the chapel back in order. They'd traveled from Boston and Philadelphia respectively the day before. It had been over fifteen years since Maggie had seen them. She and Ross had gone to Boston when Ross's mother had died, a trip filled with lost memories, guilt, and remorse over the family not getting together more often. They had vowed then to call or visit one another every few months, but time went by, as it always did, and they just didn't do it.

"What a great man," said Will. "I can see how much he was respected and loved."

"He maintained the quiet yet steadfast way about him that I saw when he was a boy," Charlie said. "He must have been a terrific husband and father."

"He was." For the first time, Maggie fully comprehended the need to speak about Ross in the past tense.

"I'm so sorry we didn't take time to be with him more." Weeping uncontrollably, Will turned away from Maggie, embarrassed.

"People do the best they can do," said Maggie. "Ross talked about both of you all the time, but he was wrapped up in his own life, too, just as you were. Go back home, love your families, live each day as if it's your last, and let this go. Nobody can change it now." She realized how much she sounded like Julia.

Relieved, Will and Charlie walked out to their rental car and left for the airport.

When Maggie looked back into the chapel, the only person she saw was Reverend Chamberlain, slowly making his way toward her.

"Maggie," he said. "You've lost an unforgettable man."

"Yes."

"He'll always be in your heart and all around you, even when you're not aware of it."

"Yes," she said again. She scratched a tickle away at her temple.

"Did you see him here today?"

'What?"

"During the service. I saw him in the back by the sign-in book. He looked young and happy. There were two girls beside him wearing old-fashioned long dresses."

"What are you talking about?" Maggie whispered.

"Well, it's not uncommon. I've experienced it before soon after a person passes. Most people don't want to admit they've seen someone. I truly believe their presence is to comfort, not frighten." Reverend Chamberlain spoke as confidently as if he were telling a story about a stray dog wandering into someone's garage. When Maggie didn't respond, he continued. "You know where to find me if you want to talk."

Maggie watched him walk away with an extraordinary mixture of relief and fear.

Cleo was waiting in the kitchen. She sat in the middle of the vinyl floor looking up at her mistress with eyes as big as the silver buttons on Maggie's black funeral dress. A tiny meow escaped as she trotted over, rubbing herself against Maggie's legs as though she'd been absent for weeks. *Poor thing,* thought Maggie. *She's as confused as I am.* Cleo actually let her pick her up, an act usually reserved for times of minor injuries or frightening thunderstorms.

Maggie couldn't believe Spencer hadn't greeted her in some way too. Then she remembered she had purposely left him outside, not knowing how many hours she'd be gone. It was almost dark, and she stepped out onto the deck to find him. A small movement triggered the motion sensor light Ross had installed two years earlier on the corner of his shop, and there was Spencer looking back at her. He lay exactly where he'd lain for the last four days, next to the rototiller. Maggie imagined he could still smell traces of Ross on the tiller, as well as in the garden where the paramedics had examined his body. Spencer's appetite had virtually disappeared that day. He spent his time either lying in the garden, howling, or hanging his head in one of the most pitiful postures Maggie had ever witnessed. He gave no indication of wanting to come in.

"Good boy, Spencer," she called to him. "We're going to get through this together." His tail lifted up slightly and fell back down. Maggie went back in and shut the door.

After making sure Cleo had sufficient water in her dish to last the night, Maggie opened the refrigerator and gathered up some deli turkey, Swiss cheese, lettuce, and the heart-healthy margarine she had bought for Ross. *Lot of good that did him*, she thought. Only two slices of bread were left. The minute she removed them and threw the bag away, she started a grocery list. Bread. She'd add to that in the morning, although the thought of shopping only for herself gave her a strange chill. No more barbeque-flavored potato chips or maple and brown sugar instant oatmeal. No more Diet Coke with lime or pepper jack cheese. The foods Ross liked and Maggie didn't would never see the inside of her kitchen again.

She ate her sandwich, slowly, methodically, trying not to clutter her mind with useless information. Tomorrow she'd think of all the things she still needed to do. After loading the dishwasher and wiping off the counter, the widowed Maggie checked the locks on all the doors. She located Spencer illuminated by the rising full moon and then turned off the lights and went upstairs.

Comforted by her familiar nightly routine, Maggie hung up her dress, rinsed out her pantyhose, and selected a fresh pink nightgown from her dresser drawer. Makeup removed, moisturizer applied, and teeth brushed, she thought of the sleeping pills. The bottle was in the medicine cabinet. She set it on the counter.

Holy Jesus. Today had been her husband's funeral. Certainly she would need a little something to help her get a restful night's sleep. She might take two pills, just to be sure. As she twisted off the child-proof cap, the phone rang.

Cleo sat patiently near the bed, waiting, as Maggie picked up the phone on her nightstand.

"Gammy?" Julia said before Maggie could even say hello.

"Hi, honey. How are you doing? Are you all right?"

"I couldn't go to sleep without talking to you first."

"Do you want to talk about Grandpa, sweetheart?"

"Sort of," Julia said. "Did you see him?"

"Huh?"

"Today at the service. Did you see him? He was in the back with the two girls."

"Two girls?"

Julia sighed. "Gammy, I know this is hard, but I saw you looking back there the same time I did. You saw them, all three of them, didn't you? They looked so happy."

Maggie sat down on the edge of the bed, which was all Cleo needed to gratefully join her. Finally she said, "Julia, I'm almost afraid to say this, but who do you think they were? The girls, I mean."

The silence on the other end seemed as long as this day had been.

Lovingly, patiently, Julia said, "You know who they were." And she hung up.

Maggie could barely turn out her seashell lamp quickly enough, scoot Cleo over, and slide under the covers, forgetting the open bottle on the bathroom counter. The relieved calico cat purred them both to sleep.

Chapter 27

Gillian walks slowly toward the horse and wagon. No driver to be seen. "Rebeca? Rebeca?" she calls out.

"Here I be," answers the red-headed girl. "Ye sound anxious, lassie, like ye actually be wantin' to leave me." Her head drops to her chest.

"Rebeca, ye know I canna bear it that we must go off in different ways. But Mrs. Saunders told us from the start 'tis how it would be. Done with our trainin' now, and right lucky to have governess jobs waitin' for each o' us. Those fine families will take good care o' us."

Rebeca wipes her eyes. "I know ... But me job 'tis in Dundee and your job 'tis in Stirling. Might never see each other again." She cries louder.

Gillian takes her friend's hand. "Rebeca, we must have hope. 'Twas fate we survived the massacre. We be healthy young lasses with bright days ahead o' us. Though we must be apart for now, I know we'll find each other again. Like sisters, always."

The two girls sit silently on the stone ledge.

Rebeca speaks first. "All that screamin' and red blood everywhere in the snow. The chill still be with me, although spring should be warmin' me bones. Gilli?"

"Ay, Rebeca."

"Ye know what bothers me most?"

Gillian pulls her coat tighter around her. She knows the answer but is afraid to say it.

"'Tis me own mam, worryin' like she must be. She's wonderin' where I be or if I even be alive. And 'tis surely impossible to get to her right now. What her mind must be goin' through, I canna imagine."

Gillian nods. "I be thinkin' about me own mam all the time. I wonder if she survived after all. And she probably fears me dead. It breaks me own heart, it does."

"We have to write letters," says Rebeca. "One o' us could learn something about them."

"But, Rebeca, I do not have your road number, nor do ye have mine." Gillian shakes her head. "How will we ever find each other?"

"I know how," a strange voice says.

Both girls turn. A short brown-eyed man stands behind them. "Stewart, the gardener," he says.

"We see ye tendin' the flowers," Gillian says. "But how might ye help us?"

Rebeca waits quietly, hoping not to be disappointed.

"When ye each get to your new homes, write me here in Inverness. I could post letters to each o' ye if I discover your mothers be searchin' for ye here." Stewart smiles proudly.

"God bless ye!" Rebeca cries. "I feel such relief I may see me mam again one day."

Gillian's tone is serious. "What if ye take on new work and go away from Inverness? Might ye let us know?"

"To be sure, lassie," Stewart replies. "But I doubt I'll ever be lookin' to leave. I love it here, I do, and I wouldna trust anyone else with me roses. They be like me own family."

Two wagons pull up. Dread fills their hearts. Gillian loads her belongings first, and then Rebeca. Stewart hands them each a bag of scones and oatcakes. Rebeca and Gillian kiss each other's tears, gradually separate, square their shoulders, and climb aboard the wagons. Other girls are settled, waiting. Drivers snap the reins, horses start into a slow trot. Rough road. One wagon heads east, the other south. A red-headed girl and a dark-haired girl look back at each other until they can see no more.

Stewart shouts, "Ye will meet in the years to come, bonnie lasses. And your own mothers will know ye once again. If God be with me, 'tis true."

The vivid digital numbers on Maggie's clock read 4:25. She swung her legs over the edge of the bed and reached for the phone. There was no guarantee, however, that Julia would be awake. Even if she'd had the same dream, she might have woken up for a moment and gone immediately back to sleep. Julia was more at ease with their dream girls, Gillian and Rebeca. To her, they were like the sisters she would never have but somehow had always known. Maggie, on the other hand, encountered the usual complex mix of horror, joy, and fear that followed every one of these nocturnal narratives. There would be no going back to sleep for her.

Cleo, having long ago deserted the warm bed to check on the level of food in her bowl, met Maggie at the bottom of the stairs. She followed her into the kitchen, squalling frantically all the way.

"You're not going to starve, you know. I'll feed you in a minute." Maggie patted the cat on the head, thankful for the bit of companionship. Cleo replied with one final and panicked meow and then waited silently while Maggie made half a pot of coffee. When her refilled food dish appeared, the cat welcomed her early breakfast. The only light on in the house was the one over the kitchen sink. Maggie sat in the semi-darkness sipping her coffee, watching Cleo lick her feline lips and preen contentedly.

Maggie couldn't pinpoint the cause of her uneasiness. The dream? She felt a comfortable, almost soothing, sense of acceptance for the gardener who had suddenly shown up. He was almost like, well, Ross. He didn't look like him, but apparently such details didn't really matter in this mad dream world of hers. He most certainly and undeniably *felt* like Ross. And there was the other thing. Stewart had promised to resolve the dream girls' dilemma of making contact with their mothers. Was the vision of Ross at his own funeral with the two girls real? Maggie couldn't be sure what reality entailed anymore. Exactly which world was her real world?

She opened the sliding door for Cleo and stood looking out at the uncommonly still backyard. Not a single bird was singing. It was now almost five. The moon, partially covered by wispy clouds, hung low, almost touching the garden. Where was Spencer? Maggie cinched the tie on her robe, ignored her bare feet, and proceeded out the door across the dewy grass.

Oh no, oh no, oh no. She wanted so desperately to be wrong. Please, be wrong. But there he was, just as she'd suspected he would be. The beautiful, faithful dog, some time in the middle of the night while Maggie was dreaming away, had taken his last breath and left this world to be with his beloved master. Maggie, her throat closing up and chest tightening, her tears gushing onto the dry soil, knelt down to stroke his soft fur. Cleo appeared a respectful three feet away, instinctively knowing, reverently observing.

I can't take any more, thought Maggie. Ross, Spencer, the dreams—it was too overwhelming, too devastating. She wouldn't even have school now to divert her attention. What kind of life would she have without Ross and the plans they'd made? Nothing could be more painful than this.

The clouds passed, revealing the huge golden circle that illuminated Ross's garden. As it had so many times before, the moonlight offered its unique clarity to Maggie. Kneeling next to Spencer, with remnants of the dream still swirling around her head, she was completely stunned to realize that as distressing as it was to lose her husband and her dog in one week, it was the loss of someone else that filled her with the deepest, most agonizing ache.

Maggie missed her mother.

Chapter 28

"What did you say?" Gina scratched her head. "Could you repeat that please?"

Maggie smiled. "I know it sounds unbelievable, but Julia's been having the identical dreams."

"And the two of you think you might actually be those girls, or not 'be' those girls, because how is that possible—but somehow you are connected to them, you know, in a weird, dreamlike, mind-boggling sort of way? And now you believe Ross, bless his soul, might be involved in the whole scenario, helping these girls get back to their mothers? This is the craziest thing I've ever heard!"

Maggie's initial amusement at Gina's reaction was quickly fading. The women were side by side, Maggie in the window seat, Gina on the aisle, of a DC-10 pointed toward Hawaii. Convincing Gina to use Ross's ticket and come along on the family vacation he had been so excited about turned out to be a relatively easy task. Gina was more than willing to leave the cold, wet winter of Summerhill in exchange for sunny beaches and Mai Tais. Now Maggie wondered if she'd made a mistake telling her neighbor about the dreams at all, especially at the beginning of the trip.

"I'm almost afraid to ask, Gina, but what part of this story strikes you as the craziest?"

Gina slowly latched her tray table, fumbled with the buckle on her seatbelt, and eventually turned to make eye contact with Maggie. "Honey, the craziest part is that I believe you."

"No kidding?"

"No kidding. It's too freaky to be anything but the truth. Now, exactly what the whole thing means to you and Julia ... Well, that's another issue. But it seems like the light might be flashing at the end of this wacky tunnel. All you have to do is have the courage to look ahead."

Julia and Kellie leaned over from the seats directly behind. "Did you tell her yet?" they asked in unison.

Maggie and Gina both turned. "Yes," Gina said.

"And?" asked Julia.

"And ..." Gina deliberately hesitated, taking advantage of the dramatic moment.

"She believes it!" Maggie almost shouted. Kellie and Julia squealed, not caring whose nap they might be disturbing.

The flight attendant appeared. "Everything okay over here?" he asked.

"Just enjoying the official start to our vacation," Maggie said.

As holidays are prone to do, this one came to an end all too soon. Maggie and Gina sat on a bench inside the Ala Moana shopping center in downtown Honolulu, a few last-minute souvenirs at their feet. They'd had a busy day, cramming in a bus ride to Pearl Harbor, a fantastic lunch at a restaurant on Kapahulu Avenue, and now shopping while Kellie and Julia were off on a submarine ride. Tonight would be yet another luau. The first had been so much fun earlier in the week, they'd decided they needed to do it all over again. They could always catch up on their sleep on the plane tomorrow.

"Gina?"

"Yes, dear?"

"How do you suppose, with all the millions of people in the world, that two individuals can meet and know they will spend the rest of their lives together? Just look at the thousands of shoppers here. Most of them are tourists, of course, but what if one tourist met another tourist there in the Loco Boutique, and they fell madly in love over a rack of bathing suits? Or what if a man and a woman who were recently widowed but had lived here all their lives and had never run into each other until today caught each other's eyes and just knew this was a second chance for happiness? How do you think that works exactly?"

Looking puzzled by this abrupt stream of thoughts, Gina proceeded with caution. "Do you mean, how does it work that they meet in the first place, or how does it work that they know they are meant for each other?"

"A little of both, I guess. Is it all fate or luck? Do we have a tiny bit of control over our lives, or are we simply in God's hands, period?"

Gina smiled thoughtfully. "Well, that's the million-dollar question, isn't it? Is it Ross you're thinking about?"

"Mostly. When we met, the day we were graduating from college, I didn't spend time wondering whether we were right for each other. We just both seemed to know immediately and accepted it without question. It was as if our meeting was an inevitable event just waiting to happen. We never really discussed it that way, but I know Ross felt the same. It wasn't until we found each other, though, that we realized we had been waiting for that moment."

"Well, I have to agree that timing is crucial, and no matter what we do, we don't have much control over the exact moments that are meant to change the course of our lives. I grew up across the street from Tony, but it wasn't until he came home from the

Navy that we felt that sense of rightness you're talking about. It was definitely there, though, just like you said." Gina shook her head. "I still miss that man."

Maggie watched a young mother walk by with twins, a boy and girl, in a double stroller. "What about losing your mother? Does the pain ever stop?"

"Not really," answered Gina. "You know, when I was young I went through a defiant stage, thought I knew everything. But after I became a mother, I don't know what I would've done without her. It's hard, you know. You never stop being a mother to your children, and at the same time, you never stop being a daughter to your parents."

Maggie's chest tightened. How could she have ignored this for so long?

Gina wrapped her arm around Maggie's shoulders. When Maggie took the package of tissues Gina offered and had regained her composure, Gina whispered, "What is it, sweetheart?"

"My parents, the car wreck— I never got to have them around to help me with Kellie. I had to become a mother without having a mother. Oh, Kellie was a wonderful child, but still, there were days when I thought I'd go nuts. I was only twenty-three when they died. And ..." Maggie pulled out the final tissue to blow her nose. "It was all my fault."

"Come again?"

"They were on their way to meet friends for dinner in an unfamiliar part of town. I thought I knew where the restaurant was, so I'd given them directions over the phone. But I told them to turn left on Sixteenth Street and it should've been right. It should've been right! They turned left, directly in front of a teenager who was fiddling with her radio dial, for God's sake! I made them turn the wrong way just at that moment, and, Gina, I was too young to lose my parents. It's not supposed to happen like that."

Gina held her while she cried again. It was almost time for them to meet Kellie and Julia back at the hotel, so she gathered their packages and pulled Maggie up off the bench. "Listen to me, Maggie. I can see how much you're hurting. I really can."

Maggie dug around in her purse for more tissues.

"Are you listening?" Gina snapped.

Maggie looked up, puzzled by the tone. "Yes, I'm listening."

"You need to think about what I said earlier. You know, about timing and what you can't control. Think really hard about it. Will you promise?"

What could she do but oblige her friend? "Okay." Maggie sniffled. "I will."

When the taxi dropped them off at their hotel, Gina muttered something about a walk before the luau and headed toward the beach. Left with all the packages, Maggie joined a single passenger on the elevator.

She was a young woman, maybe twenty or twenty-one, of Japanese descent. Because she was in the hotel elevator and wearing a bright cotton sundress that covered the straps of what seemed to be a bathing suit, Maggie surmised she, too, was a tourist. Her shiny black hair hung to her shoulders. She smiled shyly, but Maggie noticed her sad eyes.

"Is something the matter?" Maggie asked.

"I saw you," answered the girl, struggling for the right English words. "I saw you today at Pearl Harbor."

"Oh." Maggie hoped the language barrier wouldn't prevent her from understanding fully. She didn't mean to, but she found herself speaking slowly as she answered, "That ... was ... really ... interesting ... wasn't it?"

The girl hung her head, wiping one eye with her sleeve. "I'm so sorry," she said.

"About what?" Maggie asked, astonished.

"Sorry for, so sorry for, what Japanese did at Pearl Harbor." The young woman spoke as if she was stating the obvious.

All fears of a lack of communication forgotten, Maggie dropped her bags and instinctively hugged the girl, this poor girl who blamed herself for something totally out of her control. "Oh, sweetie, you weren't even alive then. I wasn't even alive then! The war wasn't your fault or mine. It's just the way things were."

A bell dinged as the elevator doors opened. The Japanese girl managed a tiny smile before she stepped out, whether in appreciation for what Maggie had said or as a final sign of apology, Maggie wasn't sure. It was unlikely they would ever see each other again.

As the elevator continued the long climb up to the thirty-fourth floor, no one, surprisingly, getting on along the way, Maggie attempted to comprehend what had just happened. But it wasn't her own voice she heard, telling the young woman she wasn't at fault. It was a soothing female voice capable of relieving even the oldest, deepest pain.

"Maggie, it wasn't your fault."

Maggie cocked her head like a puzzled dog straining to understand.

And again. "Maggie, it wasn't your fault."

She knew she wasn't mistaking the familiar voice she hadn't heard in thirty-seven years. But still, she couldn't bring herself to accept it.

"Mom?"

Convinced she had lost her mind, Maggie looked around the elevator, secretly hoping to spot a hidden camera or tape recorder. Surely this must be some sick joke. If she could ignore the voice, maybe it wouldn't be so persistent.

"Maggie. Listen to me. It wasn't your fault that Robert Campbell helped slaughter the Maclains."

Now this was just absurd. Why would her mother bring up anything like that?

"Maggie, do you hear me? You've been brought together with Rebeca and Gillian because they identify with you and Julia. It's time to help them."

"Help them do what?" If she couldn't control the conversation, Maggie thought she might as well ask some questions. She bit her lip and waited.

Her mother's voice was clear and soothing. "Follow your instincts and it will all be made clear."

Maggie gulped back a sob. She missed her mother so much, she could barely focus on this bizarre exchange.

"Maggie, are you paying attention?"

"Yes," she whispered.

"Rebeca and Gillian need you. Find them."

Exasperated, Maggie threw up her hands. "Exactly how in the world do I accomplish that?"

"Look within, my dear." Darla Taylor's voice was fading. "I love you more than anything, Maggie. Don't forget."

And suddenly, Maggie was once again alone in the elevator in Hawaii. Had it been only a minute or two since the Japanese girl had left?

The door opened. Before realizing she'd ridden the elevator back down to the lobby, Maggie automatically stepped out, smack into a lady in a flowered muumuu and huge straw hat.

"Gina?"

"Maggie? Is everything all right?"

"It wasn't my fault!" Maggie yelled at her. "It wasn't my fault!"

Gina didn't answer, but the corners of her mouth turned up ever so slightly.

Chapter 29

Maggie took until spring before she decided for sure not to get another dog. It was possible she might be ready for one down the road, but right now she was appreciating, albeit guiltily, the sense of freedom that came side by side with the agonizing grief of losing Spencer. There were no muddy footprints all over the kitchen floor, no forty-pound bags of dog food to lug in from the car, no gigantic piles of poop to shovel up in the backyard, no mass of dog hair clogging the vacuum cleaner, and no slurpy kisses in the middle of the night, signaling the need for an emergency trek outside. Naturally, Maggie was well aware of the flip side—there were also no hypersensitive ears to alert her of strange and perilous noises around the house, no four-legged friend to tilt his head and listen to every word she said as if he understood completely, no one to force her to get outside for a walk or to throw the ball, and especially no one to greet her with the passionate enthusiasm of a child spotting a secret stash of birthday presents. Maggie was still caught off guard when she returned home after shopping or visiting friends, and Spencer was not whining and dancing all around the kitchen in pure ecstasy, an offering of a toy hamburger in his mouth.

It all came down to the fact that Spencer was the perfect dog for Ross, Ross was the perfect husband for Maggie, and how could she think about trying to replace either one of them? Maybe later the timing would be right for another dog, a beagle or a cockapoo or a friendly mutt—a dog that would keep her company but would not invoke any comparison to the ideal Spencer.

Timing. It was a curious concept that Maggie found impossible to get out of her mind since the trip to Hawaii. The conversation with Gina, the meeting with the young Japanese woman, the unexpected encounter with her deceased mother— these were incidents an organized, structured, control-freak woman like Maggie found both disturbing and invigorating. She had to admit life had become much more interesting after Julia was born, when the unexpected gradually grew to be the everyday. For most of her life, she hadn't realized, or probably hadn't wanted to admit, that organization, structure, and dependable routine could be downright boring.

Although she couldn't forget her mother's request, Maggie wasn't clear as to what she was supposed to do next.

It was spring break, a week for teachers and students to reenergize and recuperate. Claire would be free for lunch.

"Hello!" Maggie said when Claire answered the phone. "Not going to a fancy Caribbean island this week with Jack?"

"Hi, Maggie! I was going to call you. No, we're saving our money for a vacation this summer, maybe an Alaskan cruise."

"Sounds wonderful. Want to tell me all about it at lunch today?"

"I can arrange that. How about Moonstruck at 12:30?"

"Can't wait." Maggie hung up the phone, poured another cup of coffee, and looked up at the picture of Ross on the shelf beside the kitchen sink. His warm brown eyes peered directly into her own.

"I love you every minute," she whispered.

Claire pushed her plate away, a few bites of her Chinese chicken salad remaining, but no sign of the sourdough garlic toast. Her face was as red as the inside of a plum tomato. She used the clean side of her napkin to dab at the beads of sweat forming on her forehead. "These hot flashes are about to drive me to certifiable madness," she said.

Although Maggie had stopped taking her soy supplements after the latest study pointed out the dangers of both synthetic and plant-based hormones, she'd only been having a couple of hot flashes a week. Pretty lucky so far. Maybe that was the pattern she'd inherited from her mother. But since her mother had been just approaching menopause when she died, Maggie would never know, never benefit from her experience and advice, never have the luxury of commiserating with the most important woman in her life.

"I'm sorry," said Claire.

"Sorry?"

"About complaining. Jack says I should just accept the course of nature and not worry so much about it. He says it's a trade-off for not having periods. Easy for him to say. While I'm flapping the covers all night long, he's snoring away, dreaming about golf."

"You're a great friend, Claire."

"And so are you. Something on your mind?"

"I guess I'm just trying to make sense of my life. All these years I've blamed myself for my parents' car accident. Thinking it was my fault provided a reason for the accident, which made it easier to accept. But if it wasn't my fault, then what was the reason? Why did I have to lose both my parents when I was only in my twenties? Why was Kellie denied knowing her grandparents? And, of course, there's Ross. We were so looking forward to our retirement. He'd surprised me with that wonderful birthday party. We were still in love after all these years. And suddenly he's gone. I just don't get it." Maggie began methodically stacking up their plates and silverware and brushing crumbs off the table, as if that would put everything in the order she desired.

"I know what you mean," Claire said. "It may be the easy way out, but I've convinced myself we're not supposed to know the answer to everything that happens to us. At least not right now. Maybe some things will be made clear before we die and others not until after we're gone. It's like life is one big jigsaw puzzle. No matter what we do, we don't always see right away where the pieces fit together. And if we spend our days worrying about all of it, we miss out on living. I know that's what happened to me when I was trying to figure out the Bill thing. After I relaxed and just enjoyed my friendship with him, then it became much clearer."

They sat in silence while the waitress picked up the neat pile Maggie had left for her. After a few minutes of small talk about their kids and Claire's job at school, they were out of things to say. Surprisingly, it was Reverend Chamberlain who opened the door for them as they were leaving.

"Hi, ladies. Thought I'd grab a quick bite before I go across town to visit Mrs. Thompson. What are you up to?"

Maggie couldn't remember ever seeing the reverend except at church. She imagined this was how her former students must feel running into her outside of school. The reverend looked so casual, so un-reverend-like. She felt somewhat foolish and hoped he didn't notice.

"Just solving the world's problems," she managed to say.

"Quite an undertaking, I would imagine. Say, Maggie, you are planning a trip to Scotland, aren't you?"

"What? Why would I want to go to Scotland?" She scowled, finding it impossible to contain the exasperation in her voice.

"A terrific idea, Reverend," Claire said.

Now it was two against one, which irked Maggie even more. "Scotland? Can either of you tell me why?"

Claire clamped her lips so tight, they started to turn white.

Reverend Chamberlain, ever so carefully, took the bait. "Maggie, the answers you both fear and yearn for might be waiting there. Perhaps facing them will bring you some peace." He turned and walked into the restaurant.

Since Claire had driven them both to lunch, Maggie had no choice but to get in the car with her, but neither woman could summon the nerve to speak just yet. A block from her house, Maggie finally said, "Do you have any idea, Claire, any idea at all, why Reverend Chamberlain thought I should go to Scotland?"

"Well ..."

"Well, what?"

Claire pulled up in Maggie's driveway and turned off the ignition. "I've been worried about you, Mag. I made an appointment last week and talked to Reverend Chamberlain about everything you've been going through. It was confidential, of course, but I guess since he saw you today, he felt like he should say something." A deep breath ended her anxious explanation.

Maggie didn't respond.

"I'm sorry, but you're my best friend, Maggie, and I didn't know what else to do. With Ross gone and Kellie busy with her own life, I thought I needed to be the one to step up."

"It's all right," Maggie said finally. "I would've done the same thing if it were you."

"How do you feel about going?"

"I don't know. I'll think about it." With that Maggie got out of the car, peeling off her sweater as she hurried to the door, overcome with the worst hot flash she'd ever experienced.

That evening Gina called to see if Maggie would join her for a slice of peach pie. This was a welcome invitation to Maggie. She had fretted away the past several hours worrying about what Reverend Chamberlain and Claire had said and, consequently, had forgotten to eat dinner. She couldn't believe she'd actually missed a meal.

"I'll be right over," she said.

"A good piece of pie is one of life's greatest pleasures," said Gina as she expertly dished up two plates. "Ice cream? It's French vanilla."

"Oh, why not? The hell with the grilled fish and broccoli I intended to fix myself. You only live once, right?" Maggie's disposition always changed colors like a mood ring the minute she stepped into Gina's kitchen.

"Well, I'm not sure if we only live once or not, but I do know that while we're here, we need to act like it's our last day. Life is too damn short to count calories."

Her fork poised for the first delicious bite, Maggie hesitated, wondering exactly what Gina meant. But peach pie called her name. Eyes closed in pleasure, she swallowed and said, "Gina, how old are you now? If you don't mind my asking."

"I don't mind. I'm eighty-six and proud of it. I've had eighty-six years of adventures in this life, eighty-six years of growing much wiser and more understanding of human nature and the ways of the world." Her white hair fit with her admission, but her face was, for the most part, smooth and clear, wrinkles only apparent around her eyes and mouth. She noticed Maggie's obvious appraisal and explained. "Lots of moisturizer on the outside. And tomato sauce, of course, on the inside."

"I didn't mean to stare. You look exquisite for any age, you know. You have such a healthy attitude about getting older. I don't know how you do it. Now that I'm alone, I fear I'll turn into a crotchety old widow. I was planning on growing old with Ross, but now it's only me who has a row of vitamins and medications lined up in the bathroom cupboard. When I get out of bed in the morning, there's no one to talk to about my stiff back or the kink in my neck. Who will go to the doctor with me if I get sick? Ross has been gone less than a year and I miss him for many reasons, but one of them is that we genuinely cared for each other. I took so many things for granted about him." Maggie set her empty plate in the sink. "You make the best pie crust I've ever had."

"Years of practice, my dear," Gina said. She wiped up the crumbs around the pie plate and covered what was left with a sheet of plastic wrap. "I've got something I need to tell you."

Gina's serious manner worried Maggie. She sat up straight in the wooden chair.

"I realize we haven't known each other all that long, but in a way you've become like a daughter to me, Maggie. My son lives out in Michigan, and his wife has always been wonderful, but even adult women tend to gravitate toward their own mothers, pulling their husbands along with them. My three grandchildren are grown now with lives of their own. I love them all dearly, but they are there and I am here. Having you next door has been an unexpected delight. You've given me an element in my life that I didn't know I needed until I met you." She paused, as if trying to think how to go on.

"I feel the same way," Maggie said, startled by Gina's honest confession. "You clearly fill an empty hole in me, one I had ignored until recently. You are everything I hope my own mother would be if she'd lived."

"Thank you."

Maggie waited for the rest, as most certainly there was more to come. When Gina remained silent, she asked, "And?"

"It's not as simple to say as I thought it would be." Gina's voice was equally steady and anxious. "I haven't even told my son yet."

"All right, now you're scaring me. What is it?" Maggie moved to the chair next to Gina, leaning toward her like a cat ready to jump between tabletops.

"My damn pancreas, honey. It's cancer and it's going to be quick. I don't want to go through all that chemo crap at my age, so there's not much anybody can do. I didn't want to upset you, but it's going to be impossible to keep it a secret."

Maggie's chin dropped to her chest; her eyes filled, but she refused to let go of the tears. Anger kept them there, furious anger over the injustice of all the devastating losses she was expected to come to terms with—her beloved Ross, devoted Spencer, the repressed sorrow of her long-departed parents, the missing link she was somehow supposed to "fix" with the mysterious dream girls, and now Gina, the feisty, rock-solid woman Maggie had counted on to lead her into the next phase of her life.

Maggie teetered on a narrow edge, one which lacked a preferential side. She could fall back into the maddening yet strangely familiar life she'd nearly come to accept as normal, or she could leap off into the unknown, hoping to find the last pieces of this intricate mosaic that had begun thirteen years ago.

A sudden grasp of her hand made Maggie jump. "It's part of the cycle, Maggie," Gina said, an incredible strength and contentment in her eyes. "I do believe I'll be on a new adventure, in an astonishing place we can only envision. I'll see you there someday, I'm sure of it."

Maggie's lip quivered, but the tears still would not fall. The anticipation of what Gina might say next, of which side of the edge she might guide her toward, paralyzed her.

Considering the circumstances, Gina should have been the one receiving the support. Instead, she offered it to Maggie. "Honey, you have a cycle of your own to complete. You know this. You need to take Julia and go to Scotland."

And with that, the plates in the sink, still sticky with sugary peaches and flakes of perfect crust, settled with a reassuring shift.

Chapter 30

Brown horse stumbles. Dark mud splashes up from road. Blooming heather, strong and delicate. Stewart, kind eyes squinting in the dazzling sunshine, steers his horse to the roadside. "Whoa!"

Two young women, one with dark hair flowing freely around her shoulders, the other with curly red hair pulled tightly in a bun, sit side by side. Puzzled expressions as the horse brings the carriage to a sudden stop.

"Gillian?"

"Hold on to your hat, Rebeca. We'll ask Stewart why we be stoppin' here in just a minute."

Stewart walks around the side of the carriage. "Sorry, lasses. Ol' Duncan is a mite trauchled. We be tirin' the poor beast out travelin' to Glencoe in such a hurry. We can all have a rest now. Where be the apples and bannocks?"

Rebeca removes some for her and Gillian first.

"'Tis a bonnie morn, eh, Rebeca?" Juice runs down Gillian's chin. She laughs.

"'Tis true," Rebeca says. "I canna tarry much longer to see me mam. Me heart is truly poundin'. Do ye think she'll recognize me?"

"A mother never forgets her daughter. Never. And can ye believe I once thought me mam might be dead? Quite a story they will surely be tellin' us tomorrow," says Gillian.

"We have our own tale to tell now, as well," Gillian continues. "We've come a long, long way from that horrible night in Glencoe thirteen years ago, for certain. And now we be goin' back under joyful circumstances."

Rebeca sits quietly. Finishes her bannock. Oat crumbs fall onto the carriage seat.

"I hated being apart from ye for those years, Rebeca. But who knew the fates would bring us back to Skye teachin' at the same school? And now look at us, both with husbands and bairns. I hope they are fairin' well without us for these few days." Gillian tosses her apple core. Brown horse snorts, picks it up.

Stewart appears at the carriage window. "Ready to go?" He is older, tired. One leg limps.

"Stewart, how can we ever repay ye? Ye never gave up on findin' our mothers, did ye?" Rebeca touches his shoulder affectionately.

"I almost lost hope once or twice, I did. But it be Mrs. Saunders who got the letters and sent them on to me. Your mothers were lookin' for ye separately in Glencoe, just hopin' and prayin' to find ye. I put one in touch with the other and now they be waitin' there together."

Rebeca and Gillian shake their heads.

"Findin' them 'tis a miracle, for sure," says Gillian. "Too bad it took the tragedy to first bring 'em together."

"They'll be shocked to see how we've grown into women," says Rebeca. "Hopin' their health is fine enough to come see our wee ones in Skye."

Bumping, bumping. Carriage wheels moving again. Rebeca and Gillian smiling, reaching for each other's hands.

"Friends for life, are we not?" Rebeca asks.

"Ay," answers Gillian. "Forever and always."

In separate houses, Maggie and her granddaughter sat up in their beds. Through sheer white curtains, they each distinguished the translucent shades of gold, pink, and silver surrounding the full moon in perfect, endless circles. Was this moon real, they wondered, or only part of their dream? Which world was now their reality? Soft pillows and warm blankets soothed them back into sleep.

Chapter 31

The long green and white tour bus rounded a curve, nearly throwing Julia into Maggie's lap. As if recently cut from a postcard and pasted into the landscape, rolling hillsides appeared grandly in the August morning sun. The visitors from Summerhill, Washington, had argued over who would get the outside seats, each longing to be as close to the view as the fingerprinted windows would allow. Julia, a persistent and self-assured thirteen-year-old, had won the battle with her seatmate, Maggie. At least for now.

"Gammy, tell me again exactly what the plan is when we get to Glencoe," she said, pulling her thick, curly hair back into a ponytail.

Maggie sighed. "Sweetheart, as odd as it sounds, I think the plan is not to have a plan. We need to be open to every possibility there, you know, follow our gut instincts and all that. We certainly can't ignore the feelings our dreams have created in us. We'll know what to do as we go along." The Maggie from a few years ago would never have uttered the words "follow our gut instincts." Nor would she have been without a detailed, elaborate list to follow. Even more amazing, Maggie realized this was a good thing.

"I wish Gina could've come with us," said Julia. "She is such an amazing lady."

"I know, honey."

Unfortunately, Gina had been accurate in announcing to Maggie that her pancreatic cancer would progress quickly. After a second piece of peach pie the night she disclosed her illness, Maggie had handed her the telephone and sat by her side as she called her son. Then the two women gathered their combined courage and discussed what needed to be done.

If anyone had warned Maggie she would be losing her friend, her surrogate mother, so soon after Ross, she would have predicted a potential mental and emotional breakdown for herself. As it was, she turned out to be stronger than she ever imagined she could be, driving Gina to appointment after appointment; sorting out the many pills that kept her friend pain free yet lucid; reading aloud from Gina's worn copy of *To Kill a Mockingbird,* often at odd hours of the night, as the time of day became insignificant; sleeping on the cot next to Gina's bed only when Gina slept. Her son arrived for what were certain to be the last heartbreaking weeks, observed how adeptly Maggie was handling the role of caregiver, and sat mournfully, albeit in unabashed relief, as she continued caring for his mother.

But it wasn't until the afternoon Gina absolutely insisted Maggie leave her to go to Scotland that she realized how precious each day had become. To be present for each moment, to actually participate in every conversation, whether about how much broth to add to the pot of soup Maggie was cooking, or listening while Gina wondered who would first greet her in heaven—her husband or her parents—were gifts that had been denied Maggie with her own mother and father. She felt privileged to laugh hysterically with Gina over the *I Love Lucy* episode, where Lucy deals with the enormous loaf of bread emerging from her oven; and to cry in each other's arms as one by one, Gina lost interest in all her favorite foods, until finally she managed only a few spoonfuls of ice cream each day.

Gina made it clear she wanted to die peacefully alone, with only her son close by. "Even though you're like my daughter," she told Maggie, "it would mean the world to me to still be around when you go to Scotland. Since I do not want a fussy, bawling, grief-eating service, my son will be able to concentrate on selling my house and tidying up a few loose ends pretty easily. Please go, Maggie. Take Julia and find some answers. It will make me happy."

So Maggie finally agreed.

The money Gina adamantly handed over was sufficient to cover expenses for Kellie and Claire as well. Perceiving it as a strange, unconventional sort of girls' holiday, they alternated between the exhilaration of their first trip to Europe and cautious anticipation of settling whatever needed to be resolved with Maggie and Julia's dreams. Exhausted to the point of giddiness, they stepped off the plane in Edinburgh, only to discover Joey Martinez and Reverend Chamberlain waiting at the gate, grinning like ten-year-old boys who had just won the Boy Scout boxcar derby.

"I'll bet you're wondering why we're here," Joey said.

"Is it the lunar eclipse?" Julia asked casually. She plopped her backpack into an empty chair and started digging around for a granola bar.

"As a matter of fact, it is." Reverend Chamberlain held her sweater. "The Highlands provide the perfect location to witness the final moments of the lunation cycle simultaneously with the solar shadow that will temporarily darken one side of the moon, all on the magnificent, invisible ecliptic plane." He stopped to take a breath and scratch his ear. "It's a fascinating universal event which opens up endless opportunities for God's miracles."

Maggie, Kellie, Claire, and Julia stared at him as if he'd suddenly revealed a hidden multiple personality disorder. The apple cinnamon granola bar, finally discovered smashed at the bottom of Julia's bag, fell from her hand and clunked on the floor.

Joey beamed as brightly as the moon he'd come to see. "I've been working with him."

In spite of their determination to avoid any obvious touristlike behavior, on the morning following their arrival, the group of six Americans boarded the crowded tour bus. Joey and the reverend had insisted everyone postpone the highlights of Edinburgh until the end of the week. The military tattoo ceremony at the castle, the historical alleyways, which the Scots called "closes," and the shops on Princes Street would still be there, they pointed out. But the eclipse, in two days, could not be missed. They had already confirmed the bed and breakfast reservations. So now they had more than one reason for traveling to Glencoe.

Although the town of Inverness was farther north and somewhat out of the way, Maggie and Julia agreed they should stop there first. It was where the girls, Rebeca and Gillian, had started their new lives. Hopefully, it was where the mystery would begin to unravel. Even the name, Inverness, resonated of clarity and harmony.

The tall, elegant woman in the seat across from Maggie adjusted her pearl necklace. "I hear they speak ideal English in Inverness," she said to the stocky, bald man next to her.

"Should I be impressed?" he muttered, raising one eyebrow.

The woman frowned. "Probably not. But I am, nevertheless. It seems that perfect speaking skills are considered an art there. They say all proper English originates from Inverness."

Maggie was intrigued. Earlier she had picked up bits of conversations in Spanish, French, and Japanese on the bus, as well as the various regional dialects of English. Apparently, people from all parts of the world had their own reasons to view the Scottish highlands.

The gentle hills transformed into sharp, impressive mountains blanketed in wild thyme and heather, as the bus passed through

Pitlochry and Newtonmore. Sheep, sleeping idly in groups of two or three, or casually munching on patches of green grass, only glanced at what must have been the hundredth bus they'd seen go by in that week, their simple lives unaffected.

Inverness sparkled; the River Ness ran free and clear between charming brick towers and shops. It was virtually the prettiest, most immaculate city Maggie had ever seen.

"I can't wait to talk to someone," said Julia as she stepped off the bus.

After a full two hours of walking around town, Maggie and Julia had uncovered not one trace of enlightening information. Even stopping at a local pub for lunch was uneventful. Their meal of sandwiches, fruit, and Irn-Bru, an unusual orange soda, was delicious, but they boarded the bus with disappointed faces. Kellie, Claire, Joey, and Reverend Chamberlain chose to sit in the back this time, eager to practice their language skills and admire the souvenirs they'd picked up. Maggie and Julia sat up front, hoping to learn more about the history of the area from the local driver, James, a burly man with unmanageable hair and a bushy mustache enclosing three sides of his mouth.

Although it was just past the appointed departure time of 2:00, the driver repeatedly watched the open door, evidently waiting for something or someone. "There you are," he said eventually, as two elderly women boarded. They claimed the only vacant seats on the bus, directly across the aisle from Maggie and Julia.

"Sorry, James," said one lady, panting. "We had trouble making our way through the tourists."

"I was beginnin' to think I had the days mixed up. Where could the ladies be? I thought to meself. They've been takin' this ride every first Thursday for years!" He drew the long handle toward him, forcing the door closed, and slowly pulled the bus away from the curb.

"Oh, we're right on our schedule, you can be sure," the second woman said, her white bun loosening as she removed her dark brown hat.

"We wouldn't miss it, not with the eclipse coming," said the other, her words clear and exact. Her short hair gleamed silver in the sunlight as she settled into the window seat. "We're crossing all our fingers and toes this might be the trip we've been longing for."

"You are dedicated, that you are," the driver replied, guiding the bus skillfully around a narrow section of road, as if it were a train on a secure track. Grabbing the microphone he somberly began. "Ladies and gentlemen, let me take ye back to the early mornin' o' February 13, 1692, for our next stop, the stunningly beautiful Glencoe. 'Twas there, after nearly two weeks o' enjoyin' highland hospitality, Robert Campbell and his redcoats massacred the Maclains, of Clan MacDonald, for no reason other than their delay in pledging allegiance to King William. Men slain in their own homes, to be certain, but women and wee children died, too, while attemptin' to flee the bloody scene. Seventy-eight slaughtered, all told. 'Tis a heartbreak that many refuse to forget."

No one dared speak as the driver's thick fingers wiped a tear from his cheek. He gently placed the microphone back in its holder.

After a few minutes, Julia leaned across the aisle toward the two older women. "Excuse me. I'm sorry to be so bold, but I couldn't help overhearing you earlier. It sounds like you travel to Glencoe frequently."

"We do, we do," answered the silver-haired woman next to the window. Bewildered, she looked into Julia's blue eyes. "Have we met before? You seem very familiar."

"I'm not sure." Julia glanced at her grandmother, hoping for some insight. But it was Maggie's turn to sit by the window, and she had been staring at the scenery since they'd left Inverness.

Both Scottish women shifted uneasily in their seats. The one with the silver hair, her speech abruptly losing its perfect edge, said, "You see, my friend and I are hoping to resolve a, well, a problem, or an issue, as you Americans might say. It's something we've been dealing with for a number of years."

"How weird," Julia said, barely containing herself. "That's why we're going too! Ever since I was born, my grandmother and I have had the same dreams, like a continuing story, of two young girls in Scotland, well, now we know it's in Glencoe specifically, and more specifically, they survived the massacre in 1692." She stopped to take a breath. "I've been totally fine in just experiencing these dreams, but Gammy here"—she poked Maggie in the ribs—"hasn't had such an easy time of it. The dreams are disturbing and unsettling to her, and a nice neighbor lady who's about to die gave us enough money to come here to figure it all out for ourselves. My mom's here, too, and Gammy's friend Claire. They're back there." Julia tipped her head toward the rear of the bus. "And then Reverend Chamberlain and Gammy's former student Joey—he's a fancy astronomer from NASA—surprised us and showed up, as well. You know, for the eclipse and all. So that's why we're here."

At last, Maggie turned to face her granddaughter. The two Scottish women remained silent, mouths closed tightly. However, their eyes revealed pure amazement, which, naturally, Julia noticed.

"I'm sure it sounds pretty bizarre, but it's absolutely true," she continued. "Certainly you must have an occasional strange dream yourselves, right?"

"Oh, no, no, we surely do not," replied the one with the brown hat.

"Yes, yes, we surely do!" shouted the other, drawing the attention of every single person on board the bus.

All the passengers were staring and straining to hear as Julia asked, "The same dreams?"

With no sign of discomfort or guilt about eavesdropping, everyone, including the driver, held their collective breath. Kellie, Claire, Joey, and Reverend Chamberlain smiled delightedly in the back of the bus.

"Pretty much. Yes," answered the woman with silver hair.

Maggie could hardly stand it. What were the chances? Gathering her nerve, she reached across Julia, extended her right hand, and said, "Hello, I'm Maggie MacKenzie, and this chatterbox granddaughter of mine is Julia Fraser. It seems we may have something interesting to talk about."

The lady with the hat shook Maggie's hand first. Timidly, she said, "Nice to meet you, Maggie. I'm Dona. Not Donna, mind you, but Dona. It rhymes with Mona."

"And your last name?" asked Julia.

Her gaze dropped to her lap, but then she looked directly into Julia's eyes for the second time that afternoon and said, "Campbell."

Before anyone could fully comprehend their own astonishment, the silver-haired lady reached for Maggie's hand. "And I'm Arline," she said. "Arline MacDonald."

While gasps escaped all around the bus, Julia and Maggie laughed out loud.

James, who had barely been able to keep his hands on the steering wheel during the past twenty minutes, pulled into a parking area streaming with camera-toting sightseers. Magnificent heather-covered mountains loomed all around them. Grateful for this ordinary task to interrupt the intense atmosphere on his bus, he picked up the microphone and cheerfully bellowed, "Glencoe. Ladies and gentlemen, we've arrived at Glencoe."

Chapter 32

When the undeniable truth stares directly into a person's heart, no matter whether it is welcome or troublesome, a sense of liberating relief settles in. Truth, Maggie discovered, was at once surprisingly simple and utterly complex. The required timing, precise and often unexpected, was incomprehensible. As much as Maggie had longed for it, she couldn't believe it was finally within her grasp.

Dona and Arline, the two Scottish women who happened upon the bus leaving Inverness, the exact bus that Maggie and her group had decided to take only at the last minute on that specific day in August, the bus that had had only two remaining open seats across the aisle from Maggie and Julia—these were the women who would provide answers for, and receive answers from, the American strangers. Was it coincidence? Luck? Fate? Divine intervention?

As it turned out, to no one's surprise, Joey and Reverend Chamberlain had made reservations at the very bed and breakfast where, without fail, Dona and Arline stayed on every visit to Glencoe. These eight travelers, drawn together by some compelling force, filled all four rooms at the Thistle Inn. The physical and emotional shock of their chance meeting barely behind them, they gathered in the privacy of Maggie and Julia's room as quickly as they could order tea.

"This whole thing has made me extremely hungry," Julia said, dripping honey onto her second scone. "I feel like I haven't eaten since we left Summerhill."

Claire poured hot tea all around. "I'm surprised the other passengers didn't ask to join us. Some were desperate to get in on the story."

Arline chuckled. "'Tis a tale our driver, James, will be happy to tell over and over again if we decide to give him the particulars later. But at the moment, I only know part of the story—our part." She looked at Dona.

Their words came pouring out like a bursting can of soda that had been shaken up, left to settle, and shaken up again so many times over the years, it had nowhere else to go. Once begun, they possessed neither the power nor the desire to stop, Arline interrupting Dona and Dona interrupting Arline, until at one point they spoke in chorus, as if they'd spent hours practicing for an audience.

It seemed Arline MacDonald and Dona Campbell had grown up together, attending school in Inverness and later becoming pediatric nurses. Never marrying, they devoted themselves to caring for other people's children. More like sisters than merely friends, the women eventually shared a comfortable house within walking distance of the hospital where they worked. Their days were full, satisfying, and uncomplicated, until thirteen years earlier, when the dreams started. Dreams about the dreadful massacre in Glencoe. Dreams about two missing daughters. Dreams as if they, Arline and Dona, were the actual mothers looking for these daughters. Identical dreams of a continued story that disturbed, yet fascinated, each of them. Obsessed, they started making regular visits to nearby Glencoe, hoping to find an explanation.

When the Scottish women finished, their faces flushed with excitement, they downed their cups of cold tea and looked back and forth between Maggie and Julia.

But it was Kellie who spoke first. "Ladies," she said to Arline and Dona, "I believe we are about to find out why we have come together. I don't know exactly how, but I'm positive something significant will present itself to us soon. Very soon. And it will be life changing and profound."

Astonished, Maggie choked on a sip of tea. Julia and Claire giggled. Reverend Chamberlain and Joey leaned back in their chairs. Dona and Arline leaned forward.

As the six other people cut in with questions and comments, Maggie and Julia told Arline and Dona of their own experiences. In the end, when all details had been shared, each burning question addressed, and every similarity noted, Dona shook her head.

"This is all well and good," she stated. "However, all of our dreams stop short. Did the mothers and daughters actually find each other? And ..." She paused for effect. "No matter what the answer to that question, here's another. What in heaven's name are we supposed to do now?"

"There's only one thing we can do," interjected Reverend Chamberlain. And because he was a man of God, no one dared challenge him.

Chapter 33

The afternoon of the eclipse delivered ideal conditions—clear skies and a steady temperature of sixty-five degrees, which was warm for the highlands. Although perspiring after the short hike to Loch Leven, they knew the sweaters and sweatshirts tied around their waists would be appreciated later that evening. The mountains surrounding Glencoe stood in breathtaking stillness, as if expecting them. Claire and Kellie had visited a local market that morning, and had packed a light picnic of oat bread, cheese, smoked salmon, and grapes. Dona and Arline carried handmade quilts, while Joey and Reverend Chamberlain lugged the telescope and camera equipment they'd brought on the plane. Julia carried Arline's flute.

"I'm not sure why I still have this flute," Arline had explained earlier. "I purchased it as a teenager, hoping to someday learn how to play. But I never did. I must have been saving it for you, Julia."

Maggie, empty-handed, inhaled the clean mountain air as if breathing for the first time in her life. *No matter what happens today,* she thought, *nothing will ever be the same.*

"Maggie!" Arline called. "Maggie!"

Slightly winded, Dona asked, "Would you be so kind as to help us get ready?"

"Of course. I guess I've been lost in my own thoughts."

The women chose the perfect grassy site near a rowan tree to lay the quilts while the men set up their gear. Everyone ate ravenously, their full bellies beckoning them all toward a nap. But as a hint of the full moon became visible against the darkening blue sky, only Arline, Dona, Julia, and Maggie fell asleep.

"Gillian, why have we stopped?"

"I'll ask Stewart. Stay here, Rebeca." Gillian climbs out of the carriage. "No, no!"

Duncan strikes the ground over and over with one hoof. Snorts. Shakes his mane.

Rebeca scrambles out. She sees what Gillian sees—Stewart slumped over, reins still in his hands. Dead.

"Oh, Stewart!" screams Rebeca. "Gilli, what do we do?"

Gillian is calm. She reaches up to close the gardener's eyes. "This kind man wanted so much to take us to our mothers, didna he?"

"Ay, 'tis so sad. His heart 'twas surely made o' gold," Rebeca says. "But what shall we do now? How can we go on to Glencoe?"

They move Stewart inside the carriage. He's heavy. Awkward. Out of breath, they climb onto the driver's seat.

Gillian takes the leather straps. "Stewart should be buried near his rose garden in Inverness. We must do what is right."

Without urging, the brown horse turns the carriage around, trotting back the way they came. He trembles, moans as he pulls them down the road.

"Duncan's decided, Rebeca. He knows he must return his master to his home."

"But, Gilli!" Rebeca cries.

"We will look for another opportunity to journey to Glencoe. No matter what, we will find a way to see our mothers again one day."

"Can ye be certain?" asks Rebeca.

"Positive." Gillian hugs Rebeca close. "We will do whatever it takes and never give up. Never."

"What is it, Mom?" Kellie flinched at Maggie's whimper.

Maggie propped herself up on one elbow. Julia sat up, yawning. Arline and Dona leaned their backs against the rowan tree, nodding their heads. Yes, they seemed to say. Yes, we saw it all too.

Claire knelt down beside them. "Another dream?"

Arline, Julia, Dona, and Maggie looked at one another in complete understanding. "I think it's time," they said in unison. The four of them walked the short distance to the water's edge, where Loch Leven pulsed hypnotically, up and back, up and back along the sand.

Kellie and Claire stayed seated on a quilt, each with one arm around the other. Reverend Chamberlain followed Joey's patient instructions regarding the operation of the camera.

As dusk settled into darkness against the purple hillside, Julia retrieved the flute. The notes resonated clearly in the cool night air, almost begging for a response.

And they waited.

Later, no one could declare with any certainty whether minutes had passed or hours, as slowly the earth's shadow nibbled away at the brilliant moon. What remained appeared to grow larger in compensation, until the final crescent edge seemed gigantic and accessible, if only one of them had the courage to reach out for it.

Instead, Maggie, Julia, Dona, and Arline, the revealing dream still fresh in their minds, water lapping just inches from their shoes, clutched each other's hands in amazement. In spite of being mesmerized to the point of near paralysis, Maggie could not have been more aware of everything around her. She recognized the moment of truth. For as the last sliver of golden eclipsed moon disappeared, Loch Leven remained extraordinarily illuminated.

And hovering over the water, the outlines of those so familiar to them materialized.

The two girls from long ago Scotland seemed to walk directly toward them, looking as young as the innocent friends of the snowy night in 1692. A pair of older women, long hair piled high on their heads, lengthy skirts swishing around their ankles, emerged beside the girls. As mothers and daughters embraced, Arline's and Dona's hands tightened their grip.

The feeling was extremely surreal and yet as real as anything they had ever known. Gillian, Rebeca, and their mothers, having desperately called out to anyone who would listen, anyone who might possibly understand, were finally together and at peace. Somehow, all limitations of time and space had been temporarily suspended to allow for this reunion.

Kellie and Claire made no attempt to disguise their emotion or amazement. Joey and Reverend Chamberlain, their attention primarily on the eclipse, adjusted telescope lenses and clicked away with the camera before stepping aside to take in the astonishing event at the lake.

"There's someone else, Gammy," Julia whispered, tugging on Maggie's sleeve.

Maggie inhaled deeply but could not answer, as the bizarre yet strangely comforting figures suspended above the lake glanced knowingly at one another. They moved backward, parting just enough for the remaining presence to make her way to the front.

It was Darla Taylor.

Intense and immediate, her mother's love enveloped Maggie like a warm, childhood blanket. She didn't know for certain if it was possible for anyone else to see or feel what she could, or even if anyone was still standing beside her. Nothing mattered except the vision and the words that by some miracle reached her.

"Maggie, my darling daughter."

"Mother," Maggie answered out loud.

"Your father and I are so proud of you."

She'd been struggling to hold back, but now convulsive sobs shook Maggie's shoulders. Hearing her mother's voice a few months ago in the elevator had been remarkable, but seeing her now, as familiar as her own face in the mirror, was more than Maggie could handle.

Darla went on. "Sweetheart, by following your heart, you have accomplished something extraordinary. You and Julia helped bring together these mothers and daughters who have been searching for one another for hundreds of years."

"I don't understand," Maggie said. "Why was it up to us?"

"You were chosen, don't you see? You were meant to help yourself by helping Rebeca and Gillian. This is a gift for you."

A gift? She didn't get it.

"Maggie, it wasn't your fault your father and I were in a car accident that night."

"What?"

"Your father and I were meant to die then, don't you see? Although we were relatively young, passing together saved each of us from grieving for the other. It kept us from having to watch each other grow old or ill. I know how devastating it was for you, how you held it inside all these years, but it was destiny that brought the other car through the intersection, Maggie, not you."

"But what gift are you talking about?"

"You have felt guilty all these years about our car accident. Your guilt kept you from experiencing the love your father and I send you every day. Just like Rebeca and Gillian, you've been affected by a tragedy all your life. And though they made the right choice after their friend Stewart died, their decision to take him home prevented them from finding their mothers. Until now, that is. Only when you and Julia and Dona and Arline traveled together to Glencoe, the place where their lives changed, could this reunion transpire."

"And helping them helped me." At last. Maggie finally got it.

Her mother smiled. "We're always with you, Maggie. We're as much a part of you as Julia is, or Kellie, and, of course, Ross. Every time you think about us, we're there, nudging you, comforting you, guiding you, loving you. We'll never leave you alone."

Oh, God. The meaning of all she'd been through hit her like a slap in the face. Her eyes dried as she looked at the reappearing moon over Loch Leven—the same moon Gillian and Rebeca had admired the night of the catastrophe that had torn apart their families, the same moon that shone its way into Maggie and Julia's dreams, the same moon that gave Dona and Arline hope for a resolution, and the same moon that had fascinated Joey. Tomorrow there would likely be contrasting versions of the events occurring on this night of the eclipse. From their own perspectives, each person would remember this phenomenon slightly differently. But no one would be able to deny the perfect timing of essential forces coming together to permit it to happen—just like the sun, Earth, and moon on the ecliptic plane.

As more and more moonlight streamed onto the lake, each ethereal figure gradually faded. Kellie and Claire joined Maggie and Julia, while Dona and Arline, nearly hysterical with happiness, danced along the edge of Loch Leven. Maggie turned to her daughter, granddaughter, and best friend. Every one of them had played a significant part in this magical event. She pulled Julia close. "It's a wonder, isn't it?"

"That's an understatement!" Julia laughed and laughed but suddenly her expression grew serious. "I wish Grandpa and Gina could've been here."

Kellie nodded. "You never know," she said. "Maybe they were."

Claire, never without a supply of tissues, retrieved one from her pocket and blew her nose. "This was fabulous," she said. "Just fabulous."

Maggie wondered if she'd ever dream of Gillian and Rebeca again. Almost like sisters to her now, she pictured them already on their way to wherever people went when they found the tranquility they'd longed for. Their struggle had become hers; each girl's desire to be with her mother had been her desire as well. Their lives had haunted Maggie's days and nights, terrifying her, fascinating her, challenging her. And throughout all of it, even in the moments when she'd wanted to scream in frustration, she'd felt a sense of comfort and companionship, knowing the lives of the two Scottish girls were not so different from her own. Her head throbbed just trying to comprehend the intricate web that had led up to this night. Lives had crossed paths and connections had been made in ways she never could have conceived possible.

At the moment, however, she was clear about one thing—the enormous amount of love in its purest, most basic form that encircled and overwhelmed her, penetrating the very air she inhaled and exhaled. She could nearly see it, touch it.

And there was something else.

Something small but so significant Maggie would find herself remembering its image decades later as she rocked Julia's newborn son.

Between Joey, enthusiastically maneuvering his telescope, and Reverend Chamberlain, capturing as much as possible on camera—between the feet of the astronomer and the chaplain—grew a proud and invincible daisy.

The Glencoe Massacre

Although the dream characters of Rebeca and Gillian are fictional, the massacre they witnessed is based on a true historical event.

The town of Glencoe lies in a magnificently beautiful area of the Scottish Highlands. In the late seventeenth century, it was home to the MacDonalds and their clan chief, Alastair MacDonald, known as Maclain. Highland clans were generally considered troublemakers, with a wild reputation for raiding, pillaging, and cattle rustling. Consequently, the new regime of King William of Orange demanded an oath of allegiance from the clans. The strict deadline was January 1, 1692. Maclain waited until the last minute, and in addition, mistakenly arrived at the wrong location to take the oath. Since the MacDonalds were already considered a threat to the administration, the government took the opportunity to make an example of the clan.

On February 1, 1692, two companies of soldiers, lead by Captain Robert Campbell, arrived in Glencoe. Campbell's orders were to kill all persons under the age of seventy. The Maclains observed Highland tradition and welcomed everyone into their homes for twelve days. A severe blizzard swept through Glencoe on the night before February 13, but it did not stop Campbell from carrying out his plan early that morning. It is believed that at least some of the troops were not enthusiastic about their assignment and may have even warned the clan at the last minute. Of the 200 clan members, thirty-eight men, women and children were slain. Chief Maclain was among the dead, and his wife's rings were hacked from her hand before she died. Forty others perished in the snow trying to escape from the slaughter and their burning cottages.

It was not just the murders that outraged the entire nation of Scotland, but the unforgivable act of the troops turning on their hosts after enjoying almost two weeks of hospitality. Even King William realized he had gone too far, although the incident was silenced and no one was severely punished. Today, more than three hundred years later, passions continue to flare when Scots are reminded of the Glencoe Massacre. The Clachaig Inn in Glencoe still hangs a sign – *No Hawkers or Campbells.*

Information on the Glencoe Massacre was researched from the following websites:
http://www.bbc.co.uk/history/scottishhistory/union/trails_union_glencoe.shtml
http://www.rampantscotland.com/features/glencoe.htm

Glossary of Scottish Terms

For the purpose of both authenticity and clear understanding, a blend of English and traditional Scottish language was used in the dream sequence of *Plane of the Ecliptic*. The following translations may be helpful for the reader.

Scottish	English
ay	yes
bairn	child
bannock	thick oatmeal cake
bap	bread roll
bog	marsh
bonnie	pretty, handsome
canna	cannot
couldna	couldn't
da	father
daft	crazy, silly
didna	didn't
glen	valley
gyte	mad, insane
lass / lassie	girl
loch	lake

Scottish	English
mam	mother
shouldna	shouldn't
wee	small
willna	will not
wouldna	wouldn't

CPSIA information can be obtained at www.ICGtesting.com
Printed in the USA

268700BV00002B/1/P